A Boss'd Up Holiday With The Plug 3

Interested in keeping up with more releases from S.Yvonne Presents? To be notified first of all upcoming releases, exclusive sneak peaks, and contest to win prizes. Please subscribe to the mailing list by texting Syvonnepresents to 22828

PREVIOUSLY

BLACK OUT

Renzo

The air was cool and windy for once in Miami it was nighttime, and it was not hot as hell outside. I was in the hood with my brother and homeboys kicking shit in Opa-locka. Opa-locka was another hood that people feared to come in, but to me it was home and will always have my heart. I mean Opa-locka was sort of big and not all of it was bad. Well to me rather. I was throwing the dice and when those dice rolled to my winning number I yelled out, while them niggas crabbed loudly, mad as hell for losing they money. Picking up my money, my phone rung.

"Hey, niggas hol up! My phone ringing!" I yelled at them to not start the next game without me. "Yo," I said into my phone.

"Renzo, I'm not feeling to well. Do you mind coming over? I have been over the toilet nonstop, and I have been having nose bleeds really bad," Kia panicked.

"Ok, I got you. I'm coming, just sit tight," I told her.

I already felt bad for the situation I put us in, and the least I could do was be there for her. She was six months pregnant now and I couldn't leave her hanging because she already been through so much shit dealing with me. Ever since I tried to kill her little boyfriend that day at her welcome home party from the hospital, I have tried to keep my distance from her. That is until the nigga was found murdered in the house with a wife and child. Kia had been dependent on me ever since and I found it kind of crazy, but I didn't fault her for it. I didn't mind, but it was funny how all her cousins were team him and this nigga had a whole damn family he was hiding. I just felt bad for the daughter. That was a newborn, and I didn't know what type of person just kills a baby. They are innocent. The bad part about this is, I had to keep clearing my name because word on the street me and my niggas did it, but that wasn't on us. Kia thought I did it but once she heard a little innocent baby was involved, she knew I could never. Kia's baby bump was finally showing and watching life grow in her just made me fall in love all over again.

"Ok, and Renzo thank you, and no matter what, I love you!" she said for the first time in during this whole situation. *Damn she really bending for a nigga* I thought to myself. It's been a while since Kia said those words and damn, I felt it. She didn't know but I was going to come home if she let me, and I wouldn't dare stray again. I rather be with her and my child. It was the day before Thanksgiving and we were having a gender reveal with the family, something small because the baby shower was in a few weeks. Heaven and Amber had shit mapped out.

"Dum love Shawdy. I'm on my way," I told her. I hung up the phone and looked at my niggas. "Y'all, I got to slide and see Kia before going home" I said to them. Everyone said their goodbyes to me. My brother Ricardo walked with me to my car.

"You think you should be risking going over to Kia's house just yet with that crazy bitch of yours going mad," Ricardo expressed. He was more worried about Nadia than I was. He was convinced that she did that shit to Yams, and I was next. He claimed Yams only had us he was beefing with and the only people able to do what she did is her, but I didn't see it that way.

"Man, she home and I'm not staying over there." I told him.

"Yea, nigga but that hoe told you if you take yo ass around her one more time she was killing you and Kia," he said worried. I don't know why I even bothered telling hm about the argument I had with Nadia. She said shit like that all the time but never act on them.

"Nigga, she crazy but she ain't that silly. Plus, I got y'all to hunt that hoe down if she do," I shrugged said, but Ricardo was not feeling that shit at all.

"I mean nigga I'm gon do my part, but I think you need to play this shit safe until you got a fucking plan to leave the girl!" he expressed in all seriousness. Ricardo was a thinker and a planner. He hated for some shit to pop off and he not be prepared for it. He did everything as such. That's why I loved him. He always had a plan for something or way out of a situation.

"Trust me bro, I'm good and you don't have to worry about shit!" I told Ricardo. He nodded his head in agreement, but I could tell from his eyes and body language he was just too unsure and not feeling my decision.

"Aiight, bro," He clapped me up and I hopped in my whip and headed to Kia's house.

While driving my phone rung seeing it was Nadia. I immediately got annoyed. I thought about not answering it, but I knew if I didn't, she would just blow me up until she got me. She had become more aggressive lately and always wanting to be around me or not too far away from me. Regretting answering the call, I press the green button on my phone.

"Yo," I said.

"You sound annoyed Renzo," she stated.

"I'm good. What's up?" I asked her.

"I think it's time you come home. It's late," she stated again. She was talking to me like a drill sergeant and the shit was annoying. I was starting to think she knew something or had a GPS on me this point, because I knew for sure I hadn't been followed.

"Nadia, I'm your nigga, not one of your workers. I will come home when I'm fucking ready!" I snapped. This girl had been crossing all type of lines. It was all good in the beginning, but now this shit was pure fucking hell. The line was quiet for a few seconds, which felt like she was really listening to the background.

"Where are you going?" she finally asked.

"To my brother's house. Is that ok with you?" I sarcastically asked.

"No, but please don't be long," she advised, and I pulled the phone away from my ear and couldn't believe the shit she just said.

"Bit...!" I paused catching myself and groaned in annoyance. "Don't wait up for me, I'll see you when I get there!" I snapped and before I could hang up, I heard her say she was sorry, but it was too late she already made me mad, I hung up the phone and continued my drive to Kia.

Finally, pulling up I got a phone call from my Ricardo. We chopped it up and of course he warned me again about Nadia. It's like he was really worried, and I felt like maybe he knew something and wasn't telling me. I was the only one that wasn't fearful when it came to her. I felt like I knew her better than anyone, but of course that is always not the case either. Walking up to the front door, I rang the doorbell. A nigga like me needed to get a key because she took forever sometimes to come to the door. I knew she would give me a hard time, but some needed finessing I knew I could work to getting the key to her place. After about two minutes, Kia opened the door moving back with one of my t-shirts on and some cotton shorts that looked like panties. She let me walk in and I closed the door behind me, making sure to lock it.

"I hope you checked the peep hole before you opened this door with your ass cheeks hanging out," I complained at the sight before me.

"Nigga, you are not my man anymore. We just sharing a child that's all!" she sassed, while walking further into the house and into the kitchen. I followed behind her. She opened the fridge and grabbed some water.

"What's wrong though?" I asked her. I looked her over and notice she looked slightly pale, and her lips looked dry, and her eyes were glossy.

"I'm unsure, I have been throwing up nonstop and I had a fever earlier, but I broke it, but the crazy part is I don't have a cold," she said. She took small sips of water and went to lay on the couch. I followed and took my shoes off so I could lay with her on the couch. Her pregnancy has been so complicated. I kind of wish I just let her get rid of the baby.

    We laid down on the couch and I held her in my arms and began to rub her baby bump. I sat there reflecting, while she watched the TV. I felt so guilty for putting her in a fucked-up situation, because had I just left her alone to heal or just stopped calling and texting, shit, I should have stopped showing up on her doorstep pissy ass drunk or simply just left Sashay's ass alone, then maybe we wouldn't have been in this fucked up situation. Kia had my whole heart and no matter what I did, I just couldn't shake her, and now we are bringing a child in the world. We laid there for a few minutes when she jumped up running to the bathroom. I followed behind her and held her hair back while she emptied her stomach, but when she started throwing up blood she began to panic and so did I. Trying not to alert her more, I tried my best to soothe her so we could get ready to go to the hospital. Once she was done emptying her stomach, she began crying as I wiped her mouth and tears.

"C'mon Kia, I need you to be strong. You gon be aight shawdy. Get yourself together and let's go. I will be waiting in the car." I told her. She nodded her head in agreement.

I left out the bathroom and put on my shoes. I checked my pockets for my phone to make sure it didn't fall out when I was laying on the couch. I opened the door and walked out in the night air. Walking towards my car that was parked on the side of the sidewalk. I hit the button and was reaching for the door handle. Feeling a sharp pain hit my head and another blow to the side of my face, I fell back, and everything went black.

*****

Feeling my head thumping in excruciating pain, I tried to move my hands to my head and realized they were tied behind my back. Feeling of nervousness came over me as I began to shake and move in the chair. I then realized my feet was tied to the chair as well. Opening my eyes all I saw was darkness. I swear it was so dark I almost thought I was blind. I sat in the darkness listening, trying to see if I could hear any familiar sounds like cars on the outside but it was complete silence. At this point I had to be in a sound-proof room. I was mad at myself for not paying attention to my surroundings, and now I was filled with worry. All I could think about was Kia and if she was ok? I wanted to know if she got to escape. Or did she ever come outside? Or if she was here hurt with me? My thoughts were interrupted by the sound of a latch being released and a door opening. I heard feet approaching me. Finally, a light was turned on and my eyes began to adjust. Looking before me, I was confused but then it all made sense. Looking at me with anger I knew I was going to either die or have to figure out a way out of this situation.

"What did you do with Kia?" I asked. The laugh that came behind it gave me the chills.

"When you the plug, you don't explain shit!" Cocking the gun back and aiming it at me, I knew I was going to die and there wasn't shit I could do about it. Hanging my head low, I played the past year in my head as I began to fill with regret. I just knew shit couldn't get worst, then what I went through earlier this year but hear I am staring death in the face.

"Boom!"

SURVIVING

Kia

Slowly opening my eyes, my vision was still slightly blurry. I tried to remember what happened to me as I felt around the bed I was laying in. I closed my eyes again to reopen them, to try adjusting my eyes again. I finally turned my head to look around the room that didn't look like a hospital, but it had all the fixings of a made shift hospital room. I realized I had an IV in my arm and I could feel the movement of my baby. I said a silent prayer to God thanking him for watching over the baby. I tried to sit up slowly but the pain I felt in my side, stopped me. I noticed I had on a whole hospital gown on. I lifted myself as much as possible until I realized I had a whole thick chain wrapped around my ankle with a deadbolt lock. *What in the fuck,* I thought to myself. I was beginning to panic because now I was wondering who in the hell would be sick enough to do some crazy shit like this. Never in my life had I thought I

would be an example of a fucking Lifetime movie.
As bits of my memory started to come full circle, I
remembered Renzo. I instantly became scared,
because if Renzo was gone, that only meant I was
about to be the next victim, then I knew I needed to
figure out how to keep me and our child alive.

Trying to remember so hard what the hell
happened to me, I looked around the room and
noticed there was soundproof cushions on the wall.
I noticed a small window in the corner that was sort
of high to reach. I looked around to see what I could
use to get the dead bolt lock off my foot. Wishing
this was the time I kept a bobby pin, in my damn
hair to pick the lock. Then it hit me, the IV needle
in my arm would work simply fine. I was just about
to pull it out when I heard the door open to the left
of the room. I couldn't really see who was coming
in because the door was to the left with a wall
blocking it. I heard a familiar voice, but I knew I
was tripping because there is no way that could be
her. I heard heels and when she rounded the corner
of the wall, I was completely confused, and I felt

my anger rise. "Hello Kia," she simply said. I stared her down, examining everything about her. "I was hoping you was awake," she continued. I stared blankly because one thing I have learned is to stay quiet and observe everything, because people make mistakes and I needed to catch hers when it was made. "Well, I see you're going to be a mute, so I guess I can tell you why you're here."

Her tone was calm as she walked to the other side of the room while the doctor came to check on me, but I moved the minute the lady touched me. She tried to smile to soothe me, but the mug I wore made her take a step back.

"Well, you may want to take the medical care, because you were bleeding, and she was able to get you stable and make sure the little child your carrying will live. So, depending on how Renzo moves, your child will live, but you will die. So, enjoy your last days here. The child is the only concern since the baby means the word to little ol Renzo." She made me cringe at the thought of her trying to take my baby. I really wanted to know if

Renzo was ok. Even though I should be worried about myself, all I could think of was him and my unborn child. I wasn't sure if she was serious, but what I did know was she was completely in love with Renzo and willing to do whatever to keep him or get him back for hurting her. I had to play smart and figure out what her plan was and how long she planned to keep me alive. I needed to figure out her angle in keeping me alive and if Renzo was ok or shit maybe he was in on this. My mind was so conflicted when it came to him.

"No questions, Kia? No shit talking, Kia?" she chuckled. "I guess that drink throwing shit and trying to beat me up is out the question huh?" she antagonized me. I sat still just observing her movements, watching how she carelessly carried the gun in the small of her back, how she had a pen in her hand, how she moved carelessly in front of me not thinking I would pounce. At this moment she was right because I needed to scope out the doctor and routine, because one thing for sure, I knew how to survive and no bitch who had shit handed to her all her life was going to put me down without a fight of a lifetime.

"Damn the cat really got your tongue? Well since you don't want to talk, you can sit in this shit for the rest of the day alone and fucking hungry!" she snapped.

"But she is pregnant. That's not going to help her in her condition. She is high risked," the doctor expressed.

"I don't fucking care. It ain't my baby. I just killed a mother and daughter. Who the fuck is she? Do what I ask and pay you for, just keep the damn baby alive," she carelessly said. This bitch was a looney for sure.

"I can't do that if you starve her," the doctor firmly said. I knew then I could easily persuade her to help me.

"Fine, feed the bitch through a feeding tube or some shit. I don't know, but figure that shit out and hurry up so I can lock this bitch in for the night," Nadia said and stormed out. I could tell I was at the bottom of a house because she sounded like she was going up stairs, not down them.

"Look, you're high risk and it seems like you're experiencing preeclampsia. I'm just here to make sure the baby makes it. I can't tell you to calm down, but you look real smart so always look at the corners and pay attention to everything." Her eyes darted upward making me look to see that there were cameras watching me. She then rubbed her ear.

"Things are definitely what they seem, but relax and your baby will at least make it," she spoke in code, and I figured she was trying to tell me they could hear me too. I felt like I was in the twilight zone. "Look, just relax for now. I will bring you something light and healthy to eat for your blood pressure and I will monitor you consistently to be sure you deliver a healthy baby."

She tried to smile in a fucked-up situation. I didn't crack one smile with her. I was planning my exit because little did, she know she was dying too. She became my enemy once she allowed for this shit too happen to me. She tried to touch me again and I moved.

"Listen, I just want to check your blood pressure and that's it. I promise," she tried to convince me. I didn't want her or anyone touching me. I wanted to be alone so I could think in peace. "Fine, I will come back later," she sighed deeply feeling defeated. Soon as she walked away and left the room, I sat there and took a deep breath. I didn't know how I was getting out of this one, but I knew for sure on my unborn child's life we both were making it out even if I had to fight my way out of this shit. I laid back on the bed, to calm my nerves and it's like instantly my memory started to come back to me.

The thoughts of walking to the door seeing Renzo being dragged. I struggled to get to my gun, as I felt a sharp pain in my stomach. I tried to reach my bedroom only to feel someone quickly stab me in the neck, making me pass out. After thinking about what happened, I immediately felt my neck looking for a scar that was not there from the small needle. I let the tears fall as I began to say the Lord's Prayer for my baby, Renzo and myself. I knew this shit was about to get real, but I was about to thug it out. I still had three months before my baby was to be born and I was going to do it with my family on everything I love.

WORRIED LOVE

Renzo

Day One

The fact I was still breathing made me thank God. I couldn't believe this crazy bitch did this silly shit. She sent a warning shot that grazed my arm. She was angry, but I just didn't understand how she even found out about Kia. I planned on keeping it a secret until the baby got here. As selfish as it may sound, but that was my damn plan. Shit I was trying to figure out how she even knew where the girl stayed.

"Renzy baby, so you don't have shit to say about how the fuck you are moving?" Her tone made my skin crawl it had psychotic all in it. This girl was crazy, and my brother warned me over and over about her ass. I want to know why the nigga didn't say the bitch was real life crazy. I thought he meant like Kia crazy; This shit was mental house crazy.

"Nadia, just let Kia go. She has nothing to do with this shit. It's me you got the problem wit," I pleaded. I didn't care what I needed to do to keep Kia alive. At this point I needed to try anything. Honestly, I wasn't sure if she was really alive, but I knew she was about to tell me based off what I just asked her.

"Damn, I almost killed you and you still worried about her?" I felt the pistol hit my face making my head swing to the right swiftly. I could feel my face swelling up as I spit the blood out of my mouth. "Really Renzy? I'm your bitch not her! I will never be good enough for you will I?" she sniffed.

I looked up at her and I could see the hurt laced in her eyes like a red eyed demon. She stood in front of me staring at me like she was looking for me to say something.

"Renzo, if you want your child to live, then you will have to work for me now! I need you to move yours and Yam's product in a week. My money for your baby," she simply said. I was confused as hell because the baby wasn't even due yet, and I instantly became scared because if she had the baby, what happened to Kia?

"So how do you expect me to do that when they think I bodied that nigga?"

"He's dead. They need money and you're the only one that's supplying so make them listen. I killed him he cost me money and you're next if you don't move my shit," she calmly spoke. There was no soul in Nadia's eyes. If this was the person people were referring too, I could honestly understand why people feared her. I wasn't even soulless. She looked empty on the inside.

"Get this piece of shit out of my face and be sure to give him the drop location." She advised her bodyguards. "Renzo you have one week to move all this work, and then I will make sure you get your baby" she simply said, as if it was an easy business transaction. I knew at this moment she was not going to make this easy for me. With Yams being dead, I was going to have to fight harder in proving my innocence. On top of that, I had to move his dope with a whole team who probably wanted revenge. I heard her heels hit the ground as she walked out. I felt something go over my head making everything go dark. I was hit in the head with something hard, which knocked me out cold.

My body jumped as I leaped up in the bed. Looking around I notice I was in Kia's house. I looked down and noticed my clothes were stained with dried up blood. I got out of the bed hoping that what happened earlier was all a dream. I walked outside the room and looked for Kia around the house and of course nothing. I walked in the kitchen and there was a note with the address and time. My fears returned. This was real as it gets. I needed to do everything in my power to get Kia back. I reached in my pockets and my phones were both there, cracked screens but working. Picking up my phone I hit up Mack.

"Yo, I need you. I'm at Kia crib," my voice was weak for the first time ever in life.

"Nigga everything ok?" His voice was alarming, letting me know he was down for whatever I needed.

"Just get here nigga and bring Chase and Ricardo." I told him before disconnecting the call. I walked around the house looking at everything. I could tell there was a struggle in the hallway from the way the rug was dragged. I opened one of the guest bedroom doors and to my surprise, she already had decorated the baby's room. It was all neutral colors because we were unsure of what she was having yet. Damn, a nigga felt helpless. I sat in the rocking chair praying that I could just get her back once to tell her how much I love and miss her. You never really understood how much someone meant until something bad happened or if they died. I was feeling every emotion, but revenge was at the top of my list. I knew after today there was no room for feeling sorry, or sadness. It was time to get on my animal shit. First thing first, I needed to figure out if Kia was alive and if the baby was born, then I needed to handle Nadia's goons she liked to carry around. My phone rang taking me out of my thoughts. Seeing it was Nadia, my blood boil because this bitch was real damn bold.

"What?" I snapped.

"Damn baby, it's like that?" She taunted.

"Nadia, if you not talkin' what I need to know, then it's nothing to discuss. It's about the money. Ain't no love you killed that." I dead the extra shit she was trying to do.

"Renzo, what are you talking about? You're going to have your child, so why the saltiness? It's me, you and the little baby," her crazy ass said. This bitch really lost her damn mind.

"Fuck you, hoe!" I disconnected the call. This bitch was crazy. I needed to find out more about her because she was becoming more deranged by the second. I knew once the crew got here, I was going to make my way to see Vinny. His niece had lost her damn mind. I got up and decided to shower and wash the clothes I had on. At least by the time these niggas got here, I wouldn't be bloody. I took a hot shower to clear my mind. I wrapped my towel around my waist and went through Kia's clothes because I just knew she would have an old wife beater or some old boxer briefs of mine. Just like I thought, I hit the jackpot. She had my T-shirts and boxer briefs mixed up in her underwear drawer and I found some cotton joggers she had hanging up in her closet that were mine as well. I was happy she never threw my shit away even though she had a whole nigga. I put on the clothes and went to the washing machine, washing all the clothes I had on. Soon as I headed to the kitchen, there was a knock at the door. I walked to the door, and I looked through the window and saw that it was Mack, Chase, and Ricardo. I opened the door quickly and they all looked at me sideways and worried.

"Nigga, it's too quiet in this house. Did you do some shit to Kia?" Chase said looking around trying to see where Kia was.

"Yea, nigga, did she have the baby and you off the damn girl?" Ricardo followed behind Chase with the same dumb ass comments.

"Naw, something's not right. Renzo you good?" Mack peeped the atmosphere and the stillness in the room.

"Man, Nadia took her," I dropped my head at the words I confessed out loud.

"The fuck you mean?" Ricardo frowned his face coming closer to me.

"Man, I came here like I told you Ric, and when I got here, Kia was really sick and we were going to the hospital. I walked outside to get in the car and wait for her, when I got hit in the back of the head with something..." Chase cut me off.

"Nigga, what? Who did it? Let's paint they ass red nigga," Chase was hyped and ready for a war.

"Nigga, chill. He's trying to tell us more of the story," Mack raised his voice making Chase finally chill to pay attention to what was being said.

"Look, all I know I woke up tied to a chair and Nadia holding a gun that she shot and grazed me." I rubbed my arm where I was grazed by the bullet. It's funny how I forgot about being grazed by the bullet. The wound was not big but touching the area made me flinch. I realized I needed to bandage it up.

"Well, where is Kia?" Ricardo asked.

"That's the thing I don't know. The crazy ass bitch Nadia is making it seem like she dead and the baby is alive. She wants me to move dope, mine and Yam's portion within a week," I confessed.

"What? Has the bitch lost her mind, and where the fuck are we getting the manpower to do this shit? Yams is dead and his people think we did it," Mack questioned, with his face frowned in confusion.

"I know, but Nadia's crazy ass is the one that killed the nigga. She and the nigga were business partners apparently. All I know is the bitch is delusional and I need to figure out if Kia is alive and where she is man," I said in frustration, as I rubbed my hands over my face.

"I told your ass the bitch was fucking nuts. This girl does not have an ex that anyone can account for nigga but you. You need to be concerned about what may happen once you are no longer needed anymore," Ricardo said.

"Nigga, you know something I don't know?" I asked my brother since his comments seemed more like he was being funny than concerned.

"Nigga, I don't know shit, but what people have told me. I warned your ass multiple times. Shit all of us have, but you don't listen to none of us! Nigga something happens to Kia and the baby, it's your fucking fault!" He shouted out in anger.

"Y'all just chill out. We got to stick together! Do this shit another time. What do we need to do to help?" Chase tried to redirect the situation to what needed to be done to make the situation better.

"Yeah Renz, what you want us to do? I mean if we going to find out if Kia's alive then that means you need to find out from Nadia or maybe Vinny," Mack advised. I leaned on the kitchen counter.

"Ok, Mack, you and I can go to Vinny and see what he knows. Chase, I want you to watch Nadia and her damn guards," I watch Chase nod his head in agreement. "Ricardo, I need you to find out what else you can find out about Nadia's past," I continued, and Ricardo nodded his head in agreement.

"What about the dope?" Mack asked.

"What about it? We going to move that shit, but we have one week to find Kia, because this bitch not getting one dime from our hustle and we left with nothing. So, we gon move this shit, but we need to find out what the streets talking when it comes to Yams. We need to make sure we're not connected to his death," I advised, and they all listened, nodding their heads. I watched Chase rub his non-visible chin hairs. "What's on your mind Chase?" I asked and he gave me this look that he was ready to kill and didn't like the cat and mouse game.

"A niggas hammer is ready so just say the word," Chase simply said. As easy it would be to kill Nadia, we still needed to find Kia first.

"We got to tell her cousins. They are going to go crazy about her being missing," Mack stated.

"I will tell them, but not now. Let's first give ourselves two days to see what we come up with," I truthfully told them.

"Two days? Nigga when they cool, they don't go twenty-four hours without talking. Renzo, we have to tell them soon," Mack expressed, and I nodded my head in agreement. I went to get the clothes out of the dryer and went inside Kia room to put my clothes back on. The smell of Kia filled my nose making my heart ache. I just needed her to be ok. This shit was really all my fault. I brought this crazy bitch in our lives and now I had to deal with the consequences.

I began getting dressed in the clean clothes and I started putting my phones in my pockets. I noticed the bitch took my knot of damn money too. I was so happy I didn't trust no one like that but Kia, so I moved my money a while ago on Nadia. If she thought she was getting my money, she had another thing coming. My phone rang and I noticed it was Nadia again. Getting annoyed, I stuffed both phones in my pocket and took in Kia's smell in the room one more time. Closing my eyes, I promised my baby I was bringing them both back home, I thought to myself as if she could feel what I felt at that very moment. I walked out of her room and back into the kitchen with my homies.

"You good?" Chase asked me, and I nodded my head yes.

"So, let's roll. We got to go pick up the work. Chase, I will meet you at the spot and we going to break this shit down between you and your team and the same for you Ricardo," They both nodded.

"Aiight, soon as y'all find out something let me know. C'mon y'all, let's slide." I said and headed to the chair where I saw Kia's purse in and dug into it looking for her house keys. Finding what I was looking for, I headed towards the door right behind my homies as they walked out the door. Once we were outside, I locked her house up and got in the car with Mack while Chase and Ricardo got in Chase's whip. I watched Chase whip the car out of the driveway and drove fast down the street. Mack and I got in his whip as soon as he pulled out of the driveway and drove further away from Kia's house. My phone rang again making me pull the phone out of my pocket. Looking down at Nadia's number I felt my body get hot. She was causing me to lose control every time I spoke to her.

"What?" I yelled in the phone.

"Renzo, your tone, I suggest you tone it down. Now, where are you? You are late." She demanded.

"Nadia, I'm on my way. I needed to wait for a ride since you left me with none, and now you want to yell demands," Sarcasm dripped from my voice.

"Renzo, you better make it here in twenty minutes or else, and we know my threats are always acted on." She simply said before disconnecting the call. The frustration of it all made me dropped the phone down with force in my lap. Remembering the location, I told Mack so that he could hurry and get there within the time frame she wanted.

Pulling up into the deserted location within the twenty minutes she requested. I tried to calm my nerves in the car as Mack put the car in park. I looked over and he looked outside the window all around. I could tell he was feeling skeptical at this very moment since we didn't control the situation. We could look around all we wanted, but my back was against the wall, and I had to get out and hope that every time I saw Nadia, it wasn't my last time. I got out the whip and stood by the door for a few moments. I noticed Mack got out too. He walked over to the passenger side of the car and stopped next to me. We sat there and watched a big Publix 18-wheeler pull up and whip around for us to be able to look in the back of the truck. Then a black SUV pulled up and parked next to the 18-wheeler. I watched Nadia get out of the truck and I had to admit she looked damn good. She wore the crown of boss well.

"Renzo, play on her weakness," Mack quickly said while she walked towards us.

"The fuck you mean?" I asked.

"Nigga she hurt, so unhurt her so we can get more info on shit." Mack said and I turned back around towards Nadia who was approaching us. She wore a frown. I could see the anger and hurt in her eyes and knew then what Mack meant. I needed to make her happy and make her feel that she still got me. I needed to play on her feelings like she did with everything in life.

"Renzo, never be late again, because it's vital for your baby," She spoke like she was annoyed. I noticed her bodyguards behind her but at a good distance, which would allow me to speak with her without them listening.

"Nadia, I'm confused. You keep telling me that it's me, you and the baby as a family, but you keep threatening me," I waited for her to respond, but she just stared blankly at me. "Nadia, we can't be anything if you gon keep trying a nigga and threatening me," I tried to be as sincere as I could possibly be.

"Renzo don't play with my head or emotions," she expressed and for the first time she finally didn't look like she had demons in her eyes.

"Nadia, I chose you the first time. You got to stop being crazy. Kia was pregnant before me and you got this serious. We just co-parenting, nothing more. You can't keep letting your attitude cause issues that are not even there." I tried to tell her.

"Renzo you been lying to me, why?" her voice softened, and I knew at that moment I was wearing her down. She slightly dropped her head in defeat. I looked at Mack who nodded his head towards her as if he was saying to go to her. I walked over to her and grabbed her hand, pulling her into my chest. She laid her head in my chest and began to cry. I honestly felt bad because her emotions are what got us in this predicament. As she wet my shit, I knew I had a problem. I was about to feel like I betrayed Kia even more. I knew me making peace with the enemy was only to get Kia back, so now I was about to play the most dangerous game I ever played in life. Pretending to love someone who wanted do harm to you, is the hardest shit to ever fake.

MISSING

Amber

Troy sat on the couch while I cooked the macaroni and cheese, collard greens and corn bread for Thanksgiving and the gender reveal. I stirred my famous cheese sauce to go in the mac and cheese as I turned the burner off. I turned around and watched Troy as he watched football. It was crazy how much I honestly liked Troy, but the problem was, I was in love with Mack. I forced myself to take a break from Mack because he was wearing me down. I was tempted to just deal with everything that he came with, but after he acted crazy over Troy calling me, it reminded me of why I needed to take a step back. This man was about to have another baby with Tina and the bitch was not getting rid of it. She wanted to show that she could pop out all his damn babies. I knew that I shouldn't have had sex with Mack that day at his house, but Jesus couldn't deny our connection for each other. We had too many open wounds and as much as I loved Mack, I needed to get over him. He was a bad drug habit. He was like heroin, and I was the dope fiend. Even though it's been a few days, I knew that soon Mack was going to be calling me soon. I was so deep in thought I never heard Troy calling me.

"Shit, I'm sorry Troy. My mind was wandering. What's up?" I asked as I covered the pot and walked over to him lounging on the couch.

"I wanted you to pass me a bottle of water please, baby," he smiled.

"Why are you smiling?" I asked blushing hard.

"Just happy you here with a nigga," he simply said. I bent down kissing him on the cheek and he moved his face so he could kiss my lips.

"Babe, pass me the remote," he asked me.

"So, you kissed me to butter me up, huh?" I sassed while grabbing the remote and passing it to him.

"Maybe a little," he laughed, and I threw the throw pillow at him. He laughed harder. I walked back over to the stove. I heard him change the channel, but I wasn't prepared to have the conversation that was about to happen after the news popped up.

"The family that was murdered three weeks ago in what look like some type of personal revenge. Police are still trying to investigate further, and they need your help. The wife and child were killed with a single bullet while the father Zeke Clark was tortured before a single bullet ended his life. The police are asking that if you have any questions to please contact them..." Troy cut the TV off, and there was a silent pause. I continued stirring in the pot, scared to even comment because I had been avoiding the issue and Troy has not mentioned one word to me about it and I have been around this nigga every day since we all found out.

"Amber, why haven't you said anything about what happened to my mans?" he calmly spoke. I took a deep breath and tried to be careful with my words.

"Troy, honestly I didn't know what to say. I was trying to be there for Kia, but she shut down and I figured me just being here would bring your spirits up. I didn't want to mention it because I didn't want to upset you." I truthfully spoke from the heart. I felt bad for him and Kia because despite everything, she really liked him and then to find out he had a whole family I knew she was hurt on a different level, but Renzo was who she picked to comfort her over anyone.

"I mean I felt like you as the person that is spending all this time with a nigga, like you want something serious, would at least ask me if I was ok or asked me what the hell happened? Maybe even ask do I know who did it? But that's not something you did. You came here every day like nothing was going on, and don't get a nigga wrong, it took my mind off of it, but I couldn't help but think was you the snake that caused my nigga to die." His last words hit me like a ton of bricks because I couldn't believe this niggas audacity. I frowned my face up immediately and turned my ass quickly around and marched out the kitchen towards him. Before I could say one word, he held his hand up, silencing me before I spoke. "A nigga don't give a fuck about how you feel now, because you never even asked a nigga then how I felt. Even if you didn't do it, you know who did and you sit in my face every day like y'all didn't do shit or know shit and that's the part that's been stuck on my mind heavy. Like why not just say something. Am I fucking with the opp or some shit!" His face wore a mug, and his eyes were cold like glaciers.

"Listen, I ain't no snake and what you not gon do is accuse me of some shit like that! Like nigga I can't believe you! I wouldn't ..." His loud ass phone began ringing and we both looked at it. He reached for the ringing phone and stared at the number as the phone rang. He moved slow at answering it. The unknown number that graced his phone was typical because he never saved numbers. "Yo!" His voice sounded how he looked, which was annoyed aggravated. The caller talked, but I couldn't make out what he was saying. I just knew it was a nigga because of the baritone voice. "Aiight, thanks for hitting a nigga up," He responded to the person on the other end of the phone. "Well, we gon link and figure this shit out," he paused again while the person talked. "'Aiight, yoooo," he said and disconnected the call. "Amber, call your cousin now. I swear if what the streets are saying is true and Renzo or Mack had anything to do with this shit, they both dying tonight!" He yelled. I watched him struggle to get up, getting his crutches. It was crazy that he was making threats in his condition. Like nigga one push and you going down. Calm that buff man attitude down somewhere. Standing in front of the couch, I got instantly angry because I knew how Mack and Renzo got down and killing a woman, let alone a baby wasn't something they just did.

"Nigga, that is not Mack and Renzo pace. They don't kill fucking children and women! And if the nigga kept a whole fucking family a damn secret, ain't no telling what the fuck happened to him or what the fuck he got going on. You instantly blaming Mack and Renzo. First of all, Renzo wouldn't dare do that to Kia even if he wanted to," I defended. Troy looked at me as if I had two heads on my neck.

"Girl do you hear how stupid you sound? Niggas die over respect. You don't think they will kill for it too? I hope for your sake that you telling the truth because the whole city is coming for them and that includes you and your cousins," He coldly said.

"So, you would kill me?" I asked in disbelief.

"Hey sometimes we have to do what we have to do no matter how much it hurts," his crippled ass said limping towards his bedroom. I was so mad I followed behind him and shoved his ass to the ground.

"Aaahh shit!" He yelled as he hit the ground making a loud thud.

"Bitch, sit yo cripple ass in time out and think about what the fuck you just told me. I'm going to go get answers and I swear if I'm fucking right, you and I are done on every level possible! I can't believe you said you will kill me nigga!" I ranted.

"Amber, I didn't say it. I implied it. There is a difference, now help a nigga up," he demanded. I laughed at his stupid ass.

"Fuck you. I implied you need to get your own ass off the fucking floor," I walked away as he yelled after me. I went to the kitchen and cut the stove off as Troy continued to yell at me. I grabbed my purse and keys, leaving Troy's dumb ass to struggle to get off the floor. How the hell you make threats and you just as fucking cripple as they come right now? Nigga, done lost all his marbles.

As I drove to my home with Mack, I blew up Kia's phone. I began to worry so I detoured to her house. It was very unlike Kia to not answer her calls. I continued to call her my whole way over to her house. I pulled up and noticed her car was sitting in the driveway. I pulled in behind her car and got out. I walked towards the door and put the key in to unlock it. I walked in and the first thing that I noticed was that the alarm system wasn't on. I stopped dead in my tracks and reached in my purse for my gun. I walked further inside, with my gun pointed.

"Kia!" I shouted and got no response. I shouted three more times as I walked further in the house. I paused for a moment to listen to see if I could hear anyone inside the house. After a few moments of silence and the refrigerator making a noise, I decided to check the whole house and it was empty. I noticed her purse and cell phone sitting in the chair. I grabbed her phone and unlocked it, I notice the missed calls along with Renzo being the last person she spoke with. Becoming nervous, I grabbed my phone and began calling Renzo over and over again. I was hit with the voicemail every time. I decided to call Mack and see had he heard from either one of them. Mack answered on the eight time I called.

"Nigga, I don't care what you got going on. Just answer the phone. It's an emergency!" I snapped as soon as he answered.

"Yo, man a nigga was busy. Just chill, what's wrong?" he calmly spoke, but that only pissed me off more.

"Nigga, I just need to know have you spoke to Renzo and has he seen Kia? She's not answering her phone, so I came to her house. Her alarm wasn't on, and her whip, purse and phone is here. Like I'm really worried." I confessed.

"Um, let me hit Renzo and I will call you back," Mack sounded a little weird and something in the pit of my stomach told me something was off.

"Mack did y'all kill Yams? Did something happen to my cousin?" My voice cracked at the thought of my cousin and unborn child being harmed.

"No, man, listen a nigga will talk to you in person. You still at Kia's crib?" he asked.

"Yes, but what is going on Mack?" I was now alarmed and worried. "What happened to Yams, Renzo and Kia?" Something was definitely not right.

"Aiight, I'm pulling up. Call Heaven too and have her come to Kia's house," Mack said making me more scared.

"Mack, can you at least tell me if her and Renzo are ok?" I begged.

"They are good," he said but I knew it was not the truth. He didn't seem sure of what he just said.

"Mack…" I was about to beg, but he cut me off.

"Amber just chill. I will see you in a few," Mack said and disconnected the call. I looked at the phone in shock. I began to panic as I dialed Heaven. Something was definitely wrong.

"Hey cousin!" Heaven giggled in the phone. "Omg! Stop Caleb!" she yelled out and I rolled my damn eyes.

"I need you to come to Kia's house right now. Some shit just happened, and I can't even tell you on the phone," I quickly told her.

"Amber you not making any sense. What is wrong?" her toned changed from happy to serious.

"If you want to know, pull up to Kia's house and leave yo L seven nigga," I retorted and press the end button on my phone. I sat in the empty house a nervous wreck. I got up and started walking around the house trying to determine if I could figure out anything. I walked inside the baby room and I almost choked on my emotions. I loved my cousin, and I was just praying to God that shit was good with her. I went back into the living room and heard someone jingling the handle of the door. I was so paranoid, I grabbed my gun and cocked ready to shoot who ever entered because far as I knew, Heaven and I were the only ones with a key for emergency purposes. I knew for a fact Heaven didn't get here that quick. I stood with the gun aimed at the door ready. I heard keys jiggle again and then the door unlocked and pushed open. To see Renzo's face, I sighed big and dropped my hand holding the gun.

"What the fuck, you gon shoot me," Renzo jumped back from being startled.

"I didn't know who you were, man. No one but me and Heaven has a key to here," I explained.

"Naw, you good," he said walking further in with Mack and Ricardo in tow.

"Where is Kia? What is going on and why the hell you got her keys!" noticing Kia's keys in his hand.

"Look, some shit popped off with the plug and she snatched Kia," Renzo said. I looked at that nigga confused as fuck because last time I checked; Kia wasn't slanging not a muthafucking thing.

"Renzo what you mean the plug? I thought y'all plugged loved y'all? What did you do to get my cousin snatched? I swear nigga one hair on her head is out of place, I'm going to kill your ass myself!" I screamed as I tried to get to him, but Mack stopped me.

"Chill Amber, let him finish," Mack tried to calm me down. "Nigga, tell her the truth because this shit serious." Mack snapped on Renzo, whose eyes turned red like he was about to tear up. I now started to really pay attention to him, and he look like he was beat up. Now, I was even more worried than I was before.

"Renzo what in the hell is going on?" I pleaded at this point.

"Amber, the lil bitch I was fucking with had Kia snatched. She wants me to sell Yam's dope, plus what she giving me in exchange for the baby," Renzo finally confessed. I saw nothing but red. This nigga got my cousin in some shit with a bitch who was a damn plug. The bitch he cheated on my cousin with. He got this bitch snatching and making demands on my cousin who didn't even want him. I don't know how I did it, but I slide out of Mack's grasp and started to beat Renzo's ass. Even though I knew me being a woman would not hurt him enough, I tried my best to kick his ass until Ricardo and Mack pulled me away.

"How could you let her get hurt? You better find my cousin and her baby, Renzo. I swear to God, or I will kill you myself." I yelled out in tears. Mack held me as I balled up crying. I couldn't believe there was a possibility I wasn't going to see my cousin again.

"So, what you don't get Kia back? Like make it make sense?" I asked and he just looked at me as if he didn't even know the answer to that.

"Amber on my life, I will get her and the baby back, but I need y'all help to do it," he said. I was sick to my stomach.

"Baby, I need you to be on your G shit, right now," Mack spoke to me as the tears flowed. "Cry that shit out, but we got to put our heads together to get this shit handled," Mack told me as he rubbed my back. I nodded my head in agreement.

"So, what do I need to do?"' I asked finally calming down. The knock at the door made us turn in the direction of the door. Renzo answered it and in walked in Heaven. She looked annoyed until her eyes landed on Ricardo. They twinkled at that point.

"Hey, why everyone looks so sad? What is going on Amber," she walked towards me, laying her bag down on the couch.

"Ask Renzo," I sneered and put my face into Mack's chest, as Renzo broke down everything and how it went down not leaving a detail out. Heaven tried to shoot his ass as soon as he was done with telling us what happened. It took another thirty minutes to calm Heaven down. It was so weird to see her interacting with Ricardo. I knew the look he was giving her. It was the same look Renzo gives Kia and the same Mack gives me. I don't think she knew how much that nigga really liked her, but she was about to find out soon enough. We loved Kia she was the one that kept us all together. We needed to find her and fast.

"Who is this bitch anyway?" Heaven asked.

"Girl, the white bitch," I rolled my eyes at Renzo.

"Ok, but I never seen her before," Heaven advised.

"Damn, you right, because you were not with us when we all went out. Girl I don't have a picture of her but it's crazy. I'm no hater, the bitch is pretty, but too pretty to be insecure over Renzo's silly ass." I rolled my eyes at him again.

"Look, I need all hands-on deck to move this weight. The bitch killed Yams. She's not wrapped too tight in the head, and we have to move strategically to get at her. Chase is scoping her movements out now. I'm going to meet with Vinny, after I leave from here to figure out what is going on." Renzo said.

"Wait, you want me to move dope?" Heaven's bougie ass said making me snap my head in her direction.

"Yes, bitch. For our cousin we need to handle up," I told her with much attitude.

"Amber I wasn't talking to you," Heaven rolled her eyes at me.

"Look, we have to move Yam's stuff too, and…" I cut Renzo off immediately.

"I know you will be against it, but this may help clear y'all name. Let me tell Troy so he can help. They are going to want the Revenge," I said, and Mack immediately stood up as he looked at me as if I was crazy.

"Amber, you want me to hurt you, huh?" He snapped.

"Yo, Mack chill. She is right. We need them to know we didn't do that shit. It needs to fall on that bitch, not us." Renzo tried to get Mack to reason with me. Mack sat back and ran his hand over his face. He was looking stressed. Shit we all were.

"Aiight, but Amber just know I don't like this shit," he advised.

"I know but coming together maybe the only way to get my cousin." I honestly wanted to let Mack know that we were done and thinking we would get back together was not happening. I meant that whole heartedly. We were going to always be friends though.

"Alright, so Mack, you and Amber can move our work as normal with our crew at one of the traps. Ricardo and Heaven can just handle pick-ups and drop offs and count. Chase and I will be looking for Kia, and I know y'all not gon like this, but Mack said it was the only way and I think he is right. He told me to play up under her to see if I can get her to slip up." he advised us.

"Heaven we need to send a group text to everyone canceling Thanksgiving and say we are moving it to later date," I told Heaven who nodded her head in agreement.

"Ok, and you?" Heaven pointed at Renzo "You better fuck that bitch into a coma to get my cousin back," Heaven's crazy ass continued. Renzo just nodded his head in agreement, but I could tell he didn't want to. He was mad and disgusted.

"I'm going to setup a meeting with you and Troy so we can get this shit on a ball," I told Renzo who nodded his head in agreement again.

"Alright let's get to moving, I have to go meet up with her, and y'all may not like the this but I'm going to have Sashay making the runs that is far. She has experience and knows how to handle the police." He said and even though I didn't like it, if it was going to help get my cousin back, I was down for whatever needed to be done to help her. Heaven didn't look happy, but what could we do? This was one of those situations where you couldn't be picky when it came to someone's life, and especially family.

BY ANY MEANS

Heaven

Day Two

I sat in the front seat with Ricardo as we drove to the first destination. We needed to drop off dope and pick up money. I was annoyed that I got dragged into this shit because now, I needed to let my job know I was taking the week off due to a family emergency and then I had to figure out how to get Caleb to understand I was handling a family emergency without blowing me up. He had been calling since my ass touched this niggas Hellcat leather seats.

"So, you gon ignore ya nigga?" he sarcastically asked. I looked at him and rolled my eyes.

"Why does it matter to you?" I frowned.

"It doesn't. I don't care if you never answer that nigga. I told you what it is, but only my dick is good enough for the nine to five princess." He sneered making me nudge the side of his head with my finger.

"Nigga, fuck you. Your dick ain't all that anyway," I lied through my damn teeth. To be honest, the nigga scared the hell out of me. He was so smart and intelligent, and the dick made all my senses leave. I don't know about the next person, but I need all my senses. That's the type of dick you run the fuck from. I was not about to be his victim.

"Aiight, keep your hands to yourself now," He chuckled but I was not amused. My phone rang again and this time I was annoyed.

'Yes!" I said in frustration to Caleb when I finally answered his call.

"Heaven, don't you see me calling you? Don't fucking play with me. Where the hell are you?" He bellowed into the phone. I took a deep breath and turned the knob to the volume of the radio.

"Listen, I'm..." that was as far as I got before, Ricardo snatched my phone out of my hand, and hung it up. I watched in disbelief as he powered my phone off and stuck it in the side of the door on the driver side.

"Don't turn my radio down to argue with an insecure ass nigga. Talk to that nigga later," he simply said turning the radio up as he coolly continued driving. I was in shock. I didn't even want to argue anymore so I sat my ass back and didn't say one more word. I closed my eyes letting the lyrics to Jeezy's song rap to me.

Had them other bitches mad when they seen us.

Had to match our Rolexes baby team us.

Yeah, the earth is our turf we can share the world.

Maybe even go half on a baby girl

She said, (she said,) you ain't no good, (no good)

But you feel so good, she said, (she said,) what if I could?

But I gotta leave you alone, ah.

She said I gotta leave you alone.

I, she said, I know you bad, but I want you bad.

She said, (she said), makes me so sad.

That I gotta leave you alone

Damn, was this for me, I questioned myself as I opened my eyes and looked over at Ricardo. Ricardo was a fine specimen of a man. Him and Renzo resembled. You definitely knew they were brothers. The only difference was Ricardo had dreads that he kept neatly twisted and always styled going back. He had dimples and brown eyes. He had the longest set of lashes and a mouth full of diamond teeth. I loved how he kept his self well groomed. The nigga was a neat freak and always smelled well. He was tall and was muscular in a way where it was attractive. The body he had made me want to go thank his mama for birthing him. It was his dimples that drove me crazy. He was so damn fine. I think it was a damn crime. This nigga could get me out my panties every time, but he wasn't the type of man I could spend my life with. He didn't have a nine to five with a 401k plan. I was very firm on that because if something happened, what would I be left with? Like how you grow old without a plan when you can't work anymore? Say what you want, I just couldn't deal. We finally pulled up to an area in Liberty City. He put the car in park and looked over at me and leaned over to my seat feeling underneath it for something. He pulled a handgun out and handed it to me.

"You know how to shoot?" he asked, and I shook my head yeah.

"Why would I need to shoot?" I asked a little paranoid and all he did was smile at me.

"Hey, we on some real shit right now baby girl. Everyone is a damn enemy." He winked at me and hopped out the car. I took a deep breath and hopped out the car as well, putting the gun in the small of my back in my jeans. I covered it with my shirt and my distressed jean jacket. The Miami air was dropping, and it was Thanksgiving. It's crazy because we were supposed to have a gender reveal today for Kia, I had already sent out the mass texts to cancel, but I honestly didn't know how to respond back to my aunties and momma. They were worried. I closed the car door and he looked back at me and nodded his head for me to follow behind him. I walked behind him as he carried a duffle bag. I didn't even notice him take it from the car. He knocked on the door in a way almost like a code. Someone swung the door open.

"Aye nigga's I don't pay y'all to sit. Where my bread at?" Ricardo voice bellowed through the small house. You saw the niggas scattering around picking up shit and walking out the door. The one who answered the door did an exchange for the money. I remember seeing a lot of money when I would see Kia count up, but this money was definitely different.

"Aye Ric, this damn near double. How we suppose to get rid of this in a day? It takes us damn near three days for this kind of work," the guy who answered the door complained.

"You either move it or move from your spot and let someone else push this shit instead." Ricardo's voice was firm, and he didn't raise it. I could tell he not only had the guy's respect, but this man was afraid. I wanted to know more at that point, what made Ricardo A.K.A Ric put fear in someone.

"Aiight man, I got you," he shook his head quickly in agreement. I was amused, but I was starting to fear the nigga I let taste my pussy. I watched Ricardo feel the money and then he took some out and examined the bag some more before he put the money back and lifted the bag testing out the weight.

"Perfect weight nigga. I will see you tomorrow," he simply said and turned around to face me and winked at me. This nigga knew his dominance was sexy. I followed behind him as we walked out of the house. He walked towards the whip, and he pushed me towards the trunk of the car.

"Look, watch my back," he ordered, and I did exactly that. Once he was done, he slammed the trunk and we got in the car. He turned the car on, and I pulled the gun from my back and sat it on the floor.

"Look, we got a few more stops and then we meet back with Renzo, but you not going home, so find some excuse to give to that nigga," he said tossing my phone that was powered off. I sat with the phone in my hand in disbelief. Turning it on, seeing all the missed calls and texts from Caleb. I sighed deeply in frustration because I knew I was playing a dangerous game. While I wanted to be with someone who could really offer me something in life, my pussy wanted to cream over the drug dealer. I can't believe my body has the audacity to feel this way. I tell you what I sat there and thought of the easiest lie to tell this nigga. I dialed his number.

"Heaven, what the fuck happened? I been blowing up your phone," Caleb snapped.

"Caleb, you need to calm down. My phone went dead," I lied easily.

"Well, where are you? Why haven't you made it back to my house." I could tell he was annoyed and trying so hard to keep his anger in check.

"I was handling something for Kia. I'm going to stay with her tonight. She is not feeling so well," I lied. The line went silent, to the point I thought the nigga hung up. I pulled the phone away from my hear and looked at the phone multiple times.

"Um, hello," I said because I could see he was still on my line.

"Why do you have to stay with your cousin, Heaven? It's Thanksgiving. If anything, I can stay with y'all?" he asked, and I immediately got frustrated.

"Caleb, you do know she is pregnant and real sick, and you forgot you definitely can't stay because she doesn't like your ass remember?" I had a whole attitude at that point.

"Ok, Heaven just call me later," he sounded defeated. He didn't argue back he just gave up. Damn, maybe he did change. Since my lie was legit, he really could not question it.

"No problem, Caleb it's only for one day," I expressed.

"I know. I love you Heaven and I just be worried you're going to leave me," he finally expressed.

"Well don't think like that ok," I carefully chose my words, I didn't want to sound insensitive to him or like I was around someone.

"Call me later ok," he advised.

"Of course," I sweetly said, and we disconnected the call.

"Let this be the last time you get all sweet and shit with that nigga next to me," Ricardo warned. I looked at him as if he was crazy, but I dared not to say another word. We drove around for at least two hours doing drop offs and pickups. If this what a dope girl or down bitch did, I didn't want to be one at this point. I was too tired. The goal was to push the money so we could at least get Kia and the baby back, but I had this bad feeling in the pit of my stomach. I did believe Renzo when he said he will get her back, but the way things were playing out, I knew some shit was about to go down to make the worst happen.

After our last stop, we finally made it to meet up with Chase, Mack, Amber and Renzo. We were all at Mack's house that he used to share with Amber. Ricardo been giving me the tea on Amber and Mack situation with Tina, and I must say it was a hot mess. I knew before everyone just about, because Ricardo's ass couldn't hold water with me. When he was high and drunk, he would run his mouth like a motor.

It's crazy how we even got to this point in our lives. I ended up being his realtor for a property he wanted to invest in. He wanted to purchase two triplex's and rent them out. It started off as business. That is until one late meeting turned into a full fledge sex affair. Well, at least that's what I thought. I didn't know the attraction was so strong until we were having sex with each other damn near everywhere. It was weird at first, but then it's like we developed a friendship that I respected it. The problem is, I think I found myself feeling him more than I should have. Like yeah, he has money and investment properties, but he was still in the game, and I just couldn't risk being with someone in that lifestyle. I couldn't fully give my all to a person like that. It was safer to be with Caleb and it was quite simple. Look at what Kia is going through right now, from messing with Renzo's ass. My cousin deserved better, shit so did Amber. I am just happy Amber came to her senses early. I watched Ricardo drop the bags on the table as they began to count the money.

"Where is Amber?" I asked Mack. He gave me a look that let me know wherever she was, he didn't approve.

"Leave the nigga be Heaven. He's mad that Amber went to talk to Troy alone. You know the niggas uptight because he lost his bitch," Chase shrugged, making me chuckle. We all knew how Mack felt about Amber, and this was killing his spirit because he couldn't handle Amber being around another man.

"Chase, just chill on the nigga," Renzo who was running money through the money counter.

"Naw, let the nigga keep talking shit!" Mack shouted getting upset.

"Y'all chill for real. Direct some of that energy on the bitch causing the problems and her muscle. They the ones trying us," Renzo stressed. I could tell he hadn't had any sleep. This shit was taking a toll on him and now he was looking older than normal. The nigga that once was always dressed up is now looking run down. Renzo normally would repeat an outfit back-to-back if he was hustling, but you would see a fresh face and jewelry behind it. Now his face had bags under the eyes, wrinkle lines forming in the corners of his mouth and face and his skin was becoming pale and drained looking. I walked over to him. Putting my hand on his shoulder he looked up at me with sadness.

"You ok?" I asked and he paused counting the money, and just sat there staring blankly at me for a moment.

"I mean as good as it will get for now until she is home," he expressed.

"Well, did you get to talk to the guy?" I asked.

"Its weird. Security was there, but they said he was not available, and he was really sick. One of the security guards said he would get back to me, but I'm unsure how long that would take." He sounded slightly defeated.

"Nigga, you can't let yo feelings get in the way. One thing is for sure. Kia can hold her own. We need to handle shit out here." Chase said, but it sounded like it was code for something else. Renzo didn't say a word. He just nodded his head in agreement.

"Listen I'm gon see if I can get in contact with Vinny one more time and then we just going to have to take her team out one by one." Renzo replied.

"She not letting you get close to her?" Chase asked and that was a damn good question. Her delusional ass wanted Renzo more than anything.

"Honestly, I haven't tried because every time I look at her, I get so pissed. I want to choke her out and then she always has these bodyguards around." Renzo stated as he fell into deep thought. "I see her again today. Maybe I can be nice, but I'm not sure I can play this game with her."

"You play the game until my cousin makes it home, and when she does make it home, we won't speak on this shit ever again," I told him, he nodded his head in agreement.

"Look, let's roll. Mack can get them right for the last drop to Sashay and by the time Amber gets back with that nigga, we can move how we need to." Chase started to take charge. You could tell he didn't like how things were moving and honestly time was of the essence.

"Aiight, look, y'all make the drop to Sashay and then y'all done for tonight and we will see y'all bright and early in the morning.," Renzo said. I nodded my head in agreement. I watched him talk to Mack and Ricardo before leaving out the door. I prayed that this would bring my cousin back, because this shit was something out of a damn movie and I was definitely scared shitless.

BRINGING IT

TOGETHER

Amber

I walked to the door and took a deep breath as I put the key in. I walked inside and saw this nigga finally made it to the couch. I laughed in my head at the image of him trying to get off the floor. I guess Billy bad ass couldn't make it to where he needed to go. I took a deep breath because I had to play nice for the bigger picture. I closed the door and locked it. He looked back at me, and the cold stare let me know he was still mad. Taking another deep breath to put my attitude in check I walked in the living room and sat on the other end of the couch, placing my purse and phone in my lap.

"Look, I came here to let you know it wasn't Mack or Renzo that killed Yams and his family," I told him. He stared at me blankly. "I'm not about to try and convince you, but I do know who did," which now I piqued his interest. His whole demeanor changed.

"Who?" he asked.

"His plug. The woman he went to go meet all the time." I said to him.

"What you mean? Nadia?" he asked confused as hell.

"I'm unsure of what her name is, but I do know she was fucking Renzo and supplying him and Yams." I honestly told him. He sat in deep thought for few seconds before he spoke.

"I told him that bitch seemed shady, but he wouldn't listen, because he was being loyal to her dad. He didn't want to go my route with someone else who was giving better numbers and would have given us the muscle we needed. This shit crazy." He shook his head in disbelief.

"Look, I need your help and you're about to be upset as well because there is more," I advised as I shook my right leg from being nervous.

"What you need my help for?" his attitude instantly became visible, which made me even more annoyed and uncomfortable.

"She kidnapped Kia and she is pregnant. She won't at least give him his child, unless he pushes Yam's portion of dope and his, which is way more than he can handle…"

He immediately cut me off. "So, you want me to work for this nigga? Is that what you asking me?" He snapped.

"Look Troy, this is to save my fucking cousin. He didn't even want to do this shit. She is forcing his hand. The bitch is fucking crazy," I pleaded.

"A nigga just wants his get back! I am down. I will call my boys and we will help move the weight, but we want our cut." He spoke. I knew he would be down. At the end of the day, he couldn't let Yams death go in vain, even though he was a cheating ass nigga. Say what you want but I will never sympathize for him, now the mother and baby was a different story.

"Ok, well I'm going to have him meet with you," I told him, and he nodded his head in agreement. I got up getting ready to go, and he grabbed my arm.

"Why you leaving?" He asked I could tell he needed someone because he lost the only friend and person he ever trusted, but I couldn't be a friend right now. I was completely offended earlier, and I had to deal with Kia being gone and making sure my family was good. We were all dealing with this shit differently and to not know if she was even going to make it out alive made this even harder.

"Honestly, my condolences to the fact you lost someone dear to you, but because you accused my family for this, I don't know if I can get past that, and right now they need me more and I need them. What happened to Yams wife and kids is something I don't want to happen to my cousin and her baby, so you have to know my heart in this situation. My cousin can be her next victim and sitting here with you and not my family, is not what

I can do," I truthfully told him. I had love for Troy but my love for my family ran deeper.

"You're sure this doesn't have anything to do with Mack?" He questioned. To be fair it did in a way. Honestly as much as I didn't want to be with Mack, the love I have for him was so much stronger. I needed space from Troy as well as Mack, but this situation was going to force to be around Mack and I couldn't control my feelings when it came to him. Plus, I didn't want to hurt Troy's feelings as well because you never knew when you needed a fallback nigga.

"No, Troy and I would appreciate if it ain't on no business tip, please don't bring him up again. What we have going on ain't got shit to do with him," I pulled away and walked out of his house, making sure to lock the door behind me. I made my way back to my car. Sitting there for a brief moment, I said a small prayer hoping God would help lead us to my cousin. I was made for the hardships and ordinary struggles, but this shit here was on a different type of level. I drove back towards my new place, and I turned the radio completely off. I drove down Miramar Parkway going north and made a left turn at Red Road. I pulled into the gas station and sat for a moment. I got out and went to pay for my gas. I came back out and began to pump. As I sat there minding my damn business, my eyes had to be deceiving me. I blinked twice and stared at the new AMG GLE 63 Benz truck parked and the damn girl who Renzo was fucking with. The bitch who was causing all our damn problems walk towards the car without a care in the world. I notice the bodyguards from the night we all got into that fight at Uncut were closing her door and getting in the driver and passenger seat. Just like Renzo said, she took them big ass niggas everywhere. I looked back at my gas and noticed I had ten more dollars to go. Saying to hell with that shit, I suddenly stopped pumping and put the pump back on the hook and closed my gas cap and tank door. I quickly hopped in the car and dialed Renzo as I tried to inconspicuously follow them out of the parking lot.

"Yo," Renzo said.

"Guess what? I just seen your bitch coming out of the damn Cuban Guys with her big ass bodyguards," I quickly told him.

"What? Amber, your fuckin wit me, right? You following them right now?" Renzo sounded eager.

"Yes, I have a good distance between us and there is a bunch of cars in front of me, but I can see them clear as day and making every turn they are making," I told him, while still keeping my eyes trained on the vehicle.

"Listen, drop your location. Don't lose her and remember every spot she stops too. We have been trying to tale her, but she always seems to lose Chase somehow. The bitch won't let me know where she staying at or nothing. I'm trying to link up with Vinny now so I'm going to hit you in a few. Take pics of every place she stops." He reminded me at the end.

"Got it," I responded.

"Yo, Amber please be safe. They are good at what they do, and I can't protect you from a distance." He tried to put me on game, so I could protect myself.

"I am, I promise," my voice was small because I instantly became worried. I never in life had Renzo tell me nothing like this. We ended the call and I continued to follow them everywhere. One place stood out to me because it was a realty company building and it was the middle of the night. Thank God it was on one of the busiest streets ever no matter what time it was. I took a picture of the company name and building. Then took a picture of the bitch. I sat there for a good twenty-five minutes before she came back out with the bodyguards again to get in the car and got back on the move again. We drove around until we made it some gated community. I knew I would need to fake my way in, but when I saw the same kid who I gave money to let me in the gate the first time at Tina's crib I knew I was good. He was about his paper. Now he was actually working the front gate and I could scream for joy. I thought the little boy was less than eighteen years of age, but he was older. He saw me and laughed immediately.

"$500 to know where that AMG Benz truck was going?" I smiled. He took his money and gave me the instructions and just like that I made a little friend that was going to help us get to this bitch. I was happy. For once I had a large amount of money on me because usually, I only always keep $300 in cash on me.

"I may need you again," I winked, and he smirked back before walking off. In south Florida you damn near can pay anyone to do something for you. I drove to the directions he gave me, and I pulled to the side so that I was not too visible. I took pictures of the gate from a distance, and I had just made it to see the car go inside and disappear behind the gate. I took pictures of the guards by the gate and if you asked me, it was going to be hard getting inside on her actual property. They already had it isolated from the rest of the community. I waited until I finally saw them exit again. I followed them out of the community giving me some more distance. My phone rang looking down, I notice it was Mack.

"Hello," I held the phone between my cheek and shoulder.

"Hey, you still following the bitch?" he asked.

"Yeah, we just left this huge community out here in Weston. I took pictures of every place we been to."

"Ok, cool. Look we about to meet her now, so she is coming to us. What I want you to do is park close by where you can see her pass by leaving and follow her then. We need to be sure where she lay her head at." He spoke.

"Alright," I said. I took a different route back to where they were meeting them at. I was speeding to my location trying to make sure I made it before they did. I wanted to be there to catch them leaving so I could follow them. It took me fifteen minutes to make it. I parked at a 24-hour Walgreens where I could literally see them coming out of the street that was a dead end. I dialed Mack, who picked up on the first ring.

"Where you at?" Mack asked.

"I'm parked at the Walgreens. I will be able to see them and pull out quick enough to catch up to them." I informed him.

"Cool, be ready I will text you when they leaving because they pulled up and she is talking to Renzo now." He advised me. I looked at the clock and wondered how the hell they beat me there so quick.

"Aiight," I responded and disconnected the line. I sat in my seat with the feeling of anxiety. I was worried beyond measures about Kia. I just wanted her home, but something told me that things were going to go bad. I sat patiently for what felt like hours but was only twenty-five minutes, before I noticed the truck leave from out of the dead end making a left. I slowly jumped behind the truck. I drove for about five minutes before my phone rang startling me. I jumped in my seat and placed my hand over my chest as I felt my heartbeat rapidly.

Looking down quickly at my phone seeing it was Mack. I answered quickly and placed the phone on speaker.

"Amber you good, are you riding them?" he asked.

"Yes, I am following them now on to the highway," I explained. My palms were sweaty because I was nervous since what I was doing was particularly important to finding my cousin. I didn't want to mess up. I continuously kept a close eye on the truck as I talked to Mack.

"Ok be safe and keep your eyes open to everything," he warned.

"I got you. You got to hang up because I don't want to miss nothing," I advised.

"Aiight," he said and disconnected the call. I continued to watch the car move in and out of traffic. I tried not to get too close where I was visible. I continued to follow them all the way out west, but this time to another home that was in a community but the ones that were not gated. I parked a good distance down, but you could see the cameras surrounding the home and there were guards outside the door, as far as I could see. The home sat far back from the road, so I tried my best to take pictures of the home and the number of guards. I waited for over an hour and they never left. At that point I knew she had to be living here. I had already got two calls from Mack. I decided to call him this time. I wanted to see what my next move should be.

"Mack, I been sitting here for an hour. You think she lives here?" I asked as soon as I got him on the phone. The home did look livable, but honestly for the way she acted maybe a downgrade from the Mansion she left earlier when I followed behind her.

"Wait til you see Chase pull up. He is pulling up with one of our lil niggas who gon sit on the house. You and Chase will leave together. Just try and sit tight and you already got your location on shared, so we got you. Just don't get your ass spotted," he said before hanging up on me. I shook my head at how rude Mack could be sometimes.

I looked towards the house for a few minutes and grabbed my phone. I went through pictures of Kia, Heaven and me. As I looked at pictures from her welcome home party, a smile crept across my face along with a stream of tears. We were so excited she was home and having a baby. I felt like it was low key my fault because I should have been home with her that night. I was gone as usual dealing with two niggas at the same time. Honestly, I should just leave Mack alone, because even though I knew he loved me, his baby mama was going to be a huge problem. She had hurt hoe syndrome. I looked back up at the house and everything was the same. I noticed the movement in the house but that was all. I finally seen headlights behind me and then they shut off. The car pulled close behind me before cutting off. I saw Chase smoothly crept to the driver side making me jump across the seat to the passenger side and he jumped inside the driver side to pull off. We moved so swiftly, I don't think the bodyguards ever noticed. We drove off and headed back to meet up with everyone.

"Chase let me ask you something? You think we gon get her back?" For once I wanted the real truth not the bullshit and I knew Chase would give it to me.

"Listen after reviewing what you took pics of and saw, I can give you a definite answer soon. I don't like to make promises I can't keep because honestly if it was up to me, we would have bodied everyone in that house and snatched that crazy bitch up and tortured her until she told." He shrugged. I side eyed Chase because the nigga was low key crazy if you asked me.

"Chase you one crazy ass nigga," I truthfully told him.

"No, I don't play about my family. Kia is family. She looked after a nigga and always made sure I was good even before I started working with them. She my big sister and I wouldn't dare let no one hurt my family," he confessed. I nodded my head in understanding. One thing for sure, Chase is right. He has been a part of our small family for a long time. He was a kid when he stared coming around and now, he was eighteen, and to me that still wasn't grown; But I must say, he lived a life most adults didn't live so I understood how he felt about those that took care of him.

We finally pulled up back to Mack's house that I used to share with him. Walking in the door, I saw everyone there. I was a bit shocked to see Heaven because she had to get back to her lame ass nigga before he started crying. I couldn't stand that nigga Caleb. I sat next to Mack, who was looking through his phone.

"So, when are we supposed to meet with this nigga Troy?" Mack asked. I looked at him, and for some reason my heart ached for him, but seeing Tina's name flash across his cell phone as it started to ring, made me cringe on the inside. All that love shit went right out the window as I rolled my eyes at him.

"He agreed to meet with the condition he gets paid for his services and his crew. Also, I can have Renzo and him meet tomorrow so they can go over logistics," I advised. I noticed Chase nodded his head liking the agreement. Mack had his face screwed up, and for the first time I realized Renzo was not there.

"Where is Renzo?" I asked.

"With the she devil herself," Ricardo said. He had Heaven close to him. I watched as he grabbed her hand and held it as he leaned back on the couch with his eyes closed. He wore a stressed looked just like everyone else. We were drained and we were not even close to finding her. I wished that somehow, we could just find my cousin. I sat in the chase and leaned my head back and said another prayer, because in the morning when Renzo got back, he had no choice but to go run down on this bitch, because I was sick of playing games.

WAR

Nadia

I left my new home that I purchased out west and met Renzo at the old condo that we shared together. I was meeting with him, because one I needed to know if he still making my money and two I needed to know if we still had a chance. I know it sounded crazy, because I had taken things to far, but I really loved Renzo and I just needed him to stop playing with my emotions like the past men in my life. I tried hard to ignore what Renzo was doing, but to find out Kia was pregnant and that he started to sneak off to be with her all the time hurt me. Pressure breaks pipes, so what do you think was going to happen when my pipes burst? I snapped and now while Lolita is gone dealing with my uncle's health issues, I had a pregnant woman and a live-in nurse in the cellar behind my uncle's office in a soundproof room. I wasn't crazy, I was a woman scorned and tired of being misused and taken for granted. My bodyguards sat at the front door while I walked around the bedroom we shared. My eyes gaze on all the items that belong to him laying around the bedroom. Damn, I missed him, but it was time to boss up and do what I know and that was get rid of the problem. The knock at the front door took me out of my thoughts. I walked towards the door and my bodyguards stood and one open the door allowing Renzo to walk in. I could tell he was worn down and tired. He looked drained. His eyes held bags, and his skin was dull and not full of life. The person that was always put together was now looking like homeless person in the face. I had completely broken this nigga down, but the question was how broken was he? Was it enough to make him stop fucking Kia?

"You wanted to see a nigga?" He wasn't cold, but he wasn't welcoming either. I stared at him for a brief moment.

"So, I wanted to know where we are with the product sales?" I asked him, turning off any feelings that I had for him and immediately going into boss mode. I watched him carefully as he spoke.

"Your money will be ready before the end of the week. I just need to know is my child ok and if I could see the baby?" he simply asked. I was completely annoyed that he was thinking of the bastard child he had outside of our relationship. I felt like he just wanted to have a piece of Kia and as heartless I wanted to be, I knew I couldn't kill his baby, because at the end of the day I still loved Renzo and hoped he would still be mine. I frowned my face instantly.

"The child isn't born yet. Are you really going to continue to care about a child you had with Kia?" I snapped without thought. I realized by the hope in his eyes he was only testing me to see if the bitch was alive, which only infuriated me even more. The heat that began illuminating from my body could warm up a damn room with how mad I was. This nigga had me all the way fucked up. How could you possibly continuously try me like that? "Renzo, so that's who you care about more than me? It will always be her huh? Well, let me off the bitch now because I promise you this, I will never let y'all be together as long as I have breath in my body!" I yelled. My chest heaved up and down as my eyebrows furrowed. My anger had my face a beet red. I was over playing games with this nigga.

"Nadia, why does Kia bother you so much? Kia and I were not together and damn sure wasn't fucking. You did all this shit for nothing. I was trying to help her during her pregnancy. I didn't tell you because I knew you were going to be mad, but honestly the shit happened before we ever became official. You really did all this shit for nothing. You ruined our relationship for a chick who wasn't even paying a nigga no mind and didn't want to have anything to do with me. Like honestly you lucky these niggas in here because I would beat yo ass just for causing so much fucking trouble for some shit that could have been handled differently." Renzo expressed his self in a firm way, but you could definitely tell his anger was now present and he was all out of patience with me. "If you would have asked me about her being pregnant, I would have told your fuck ass the truth. I have never lied to your stupid ass. I have always kept it 100 from when I told you I wanted to mess with y'all both. I told you after you asked me did, I want y'all both, I told your ass straight up yea. I never lied. What you can say y'all both didn't allow it and I chose you over her, so you still in competition with her even after I chose you?" He continued. There was awkward pause where he just stared at me in disgust making me feel small. He shook his head as he walked past me to go in the bedroom. My guards were alarmed ready to go to war about me, but I shook my head to let them know to just chill. I followed behind Renzo into the bedroom. I watched him pack his shit up and I began to panic. I knew I had gone too far, but I wanted this nigga not to play with me.

"What are you doing?" my voice squeaked because I was nervous.

"You think I'm really going to be with your ass after this crazy shit? Bitch, you insane. I could never be with you after this. You must be on that shit you serving. At this point you either gon kill all of us or leave us be. Ain't shit else left for you to do." He was harsh, and it was making my breathing pattern change. I didn't think this shit through and seeing Renzo in person had my feelings worked the fuck up. I needed him, but now I was losing him. In some sick way in my mind, I just knew he would be forced to stay with me. Renzo packed what he wanted and looked me over one more time.

"So, are you going to at least keep your word? I bring you your money, I can have my child and her mother alive?" he dryly said has his eyes looked on coldly.

"I guess you will have to see," I simply said. As bad I wanted to fold, I couldn't. I was going to make him work for me until he sold everything I was about to take from my uncle, and once it was done, I was going to kill them both. I no longer had a need for Renzo or Kia. Death was going to be the outcome. I watch him grab the last item he wanted before leaving out the door. I walked back out to the living room, and after standing in the middle of the condo. In the morning I was going to start the process of selling it. It was no longer needed. After about an hour of gathering up the last of my things I headed out the door back to my new home. I was no longer going to look back. I was going to get my money from this shit and move far away. I was about to sell all my uncles' product while he was down to make sure I could be so set, that my grandchildren could live without a job.

I sat at my desk inside my office as I researched properties outside of the U.S. I was thinking about moving to Canada. I wanted to be far away from family. I noticed Heaven had been out as well since the incident, but to see her approaching my office, I got kind of nervous. I wasn't sure if she knew who I was as of yet.

"Good morning, Nadia. I came into see if I could get a few more days off? I'm having a serious family emergency," Heaven confessed. She seemed drained and tired as well. Looks like the whole family was stressed out.

"Well, I understand that Heaven, but I have to be honest. I run a business and if I can't assign clients, it makes me lose clients. Do you know how long you will be out?" I asked her.

"Honestly, I'm not sure and I'm definitely embarrassed because I know I only been working here for a short period of time." She spoke. Her face was weary, and I could tell her spirits were low about the fate of her job.

"I'm sorry Heaven, I just can't afford it. You can clean your desk out," I simply said without any emotion or care. I could tell my tone and how I let her go didn't sit well with her.

"Wow, really I am the best realtor you have, and you couldn't even work with me?" She was in complete shock.

"You may be good, but you're not the only one. I will have the position filled by tomorrow. It was nice working with you," I told her and looked back down at my computer.

"You're right and you're not the only company I can work for that is doing better than yours," she tried to take a shot at me, but it was an epic failure. My company was one of the best if not the best. I watched her storm out my office as she went to pack her shit up. Fuck her and her stupid ass cousin. I continued my search while I randomly watched Heaven go back and forth clearing her desk. I never met a bitch who acted so stuck up. I laughed in my head because she was so dumb. She didn't even notice she had been working for the enemy the entire time. Once she finally left, I finished up some work and then made my way to my uncle's house. I wanted to go check on the little unruly bitch Kia.

Pulling up to my uncle's home his usual bodyguards that sat outside waived at me as we drove inside the gate. I always loved my uncle's house. I just hated his wife. She always felt like she was entitled to the life she was married into. I walked inside and my bodyguards stayed at the door. There was really no one in the home but the front gate guards and front door guards. No one really came into the main house because for one, it was empty right now and two, the guards occupied the guest quarters. I walked to my uncle's office and went to the door that led to the room I had Kia in. I could hear the movement of the bed as soon as I bent the corner. She was sitting up staring at me. I notice the nurse I hired sitting in the lounge chair reading a book.

"How is the baby doing?" I asked the nurse.

"Don't fucking ask about my child." Kia snapped.

"Hmph, if I were you, I would shut the fuck up before you and that bastard baby be dead," I snapped right back at her. I could hear the nurse gulp while Kia minded her manners and did exactly what I said and that was shut the fuck up. Kia mugged the hell out of me, and I rolled my eyes.

"The baby is ok but keeping her pressure under control has been an issue. Her and the baby are stressed. I have tried to keep her in good health, but she is going to need a hospital." The nurse said with much concern.

"Well, figure out what you need to do. I can't have the bitch dying before it's fucking time." I harshly spoke. I took my phone and snapped a picture of Kia, looking stressed, tired and drained. I sent it to Renzo, so it could give him the ammunition he needed it to continue pushing my dope. I smiled inwardly how now she had to abide by my rules. It was finally good to see this bitch humble.

"I will try my best. I'm going to go get her food and I will be right back," The nurse stated as she headed for the door. I got comfortable, and sat in the chair the nurse was in.

"So, Kia are we quietly humble now?" I taunted.

"Bitch, please uncuff my leg and let's see how humble I can be. I bet I can beat your ass pregnant," the loose mouth ass bitch barked.

"Hmm just tone it down a little. Especially when I can put a bullet in your head without a second thought. So, you know Renzo thinks he really can save you? You should have seen when I promised him, I will let you go, but let me tell you a secret," I looked around as if someone could hear me and then I whispered. "I'm going to kill all three of you," I laughed. I watched the color from her face drain, and her heart monitor started going off. I got up laughing, not really caring if she did die honestly. I took enough pictures of her ass to give me a few days. The nurse came in with a healthy dinner prepared. She sat the food tray on the table and ran over to Kia, who immediately laid down and looked like she was about to pass out.

"What happened?" the nurse panicked, but I didn't give a fuck. I headed up the steps and exited the soundproof room closing the door. I walked out of my uncle's office and headed towards the front door when the surprise of a lifetime, knocked the wind out of me. I was so stuck seeing her face.

"Well, hello Nadia, why are you in my home and your uncle is on his death bed?" Lolita's attitude was evident and seeing Crown come inside made me even nervous, because that meant they were here to stay. How the hell was I going to be able to keep my secret a secret.

"Well, you know I'm helping move his dope," I tried to mask my nervousness.

"So, you're in my home to do it? I thought we had things settled for the distribution. Why are you not letting me know what you are doing? Where is the profits? I know Crown does all drop offs and pick-ups. Why haven't you contact him?" Lolita continued to throw question after question at me.

"Lolita, I have been running my uncle's affairs for his entire legit and illegitimate businesses for a long time. I can handle things without you and Crown." I felt insulted.

"Little girl, while your uncle is down, I make the fucking rules and far as I'm concerned, nothing changes. While I go have a talk with Crown and we see how much has been distributed and the payments, you better have my husband's money or dope accounted for." She seethed walking away.

"Well, just so you know I will be staying. My friend is here too," I said behind her back.

"Good, because we have to go over some family matters for your uncle and how things will go from now on. Send your friend home, I don't like company," she said before bending the corner to go to her bedroom. I watch Crown mug me, which never ever happens.

"Well, what did I do to you?" I sassed. I tried my best to be as normal as possible. Crown and I never had a bad relationship, but the demeanor he was giving me was definitely not normal.

"I mean, something is off about you, and it's really weird you're here when you hate Ms. Lolita. You are giving me a bad vibe Nadia, then you got these two niggas here. I don't know what you're up to, but it will present itself." He simply said heading in the direction of his room. He was one of the only bodyguards that could sleep in the main house. I quickly ran back to my uncle's office and walked in the room that Kia was held in making sure to close the door, so it wouldn't seem odd.

"Is she stable?" I asked the nurse who nodded her head. Kia looked like she was peacefully sleeping.

"I had to give her a light sedative to calm her down. But she shall be fine," The nurse said.

"Listen, Lolita is back, and she thinks you're my friend. I'm going to relieve you for tonight, but you have to come back in the morning, I will be here to greet you," I told the nurse. She nodded her head in agreement.

"Well, she has enough food on her tray, but she may be out for a while." She advised me and I nodded my head in understanding. We both headed out of the room and quietly closing the door and locking it. I pulled the drapery over that hid the door and we walked out of the office together just in time to see Crown coming around the corner. He eyed us suspiciously.

"Did you just come out of Vinny's office?" he asked as he opened the door not seeing anything out of the ordinary, he closed the door back. I shook my head no as he looked us up and down giving us both a suspicious look before he slowly walked off.

"C'mon, let's grab your things so you can leave," I said to her. Once she grabbed her things, I showed her out the door and as I headed back to the den area, I noticed Lolita was sitting where my uncle will usually sit. This bitch really thought she was him. She never ran a drug business in her life but felt like she could now.

"I need to see Renzo and Kia tomorrow," she stated.

"Why? I'm the one that handles all distribution. There is no need for them, and Kia is no longer with us." I was baffled at why the sudden interest.

"I wasn't asking you, I was telling you. I was given specific orders from your uncle, so either you deliver the message or Crown will do it." Her words were final as she got up and walked away with her head high like she was that bitch. I couldn't stand the sight of her, but I could never hate and say that she wasn't a beautiful black woman. She definitely was, but she came from nothing and now she felt like she was that bitch, which just irritated the hell out of me.

I walked out of the den area, and I had plans on staying in the house, but I needed to put pressure on Renzo to get me my money by tomorrow so that I could leave out the country. I took so much of my uncles' dope and had Renzo to flip it so that I could have enough to set me up for good, but with Lolita coming back to soon interrupting my plan, I knew I would have to finesse the situation. I knew my uncle would be down for a while. I just needed to make and flip as much money as possible before I left. Stealing from family was a big dishonor, but I knew my uncle's wife was going to do something to stop my money flow and the way I ran shit. I needed the money so I could disappear after I did what I needed to do. Lolita always hated me, and I honestly didn't understand or know why. I never really did anything to the lady but handle business for my uncle. I needed to make a little more to get me straight, but I would have to settle for what I would take from what Renzo made, plus what I already had. I knew I would still be straight way after death. Plus, I knew how to sell homes like it was dope. I left the house and made my way to my home. I needed to call Renzo and add pressure to him to get him to push this dope faster. My time was running out and I refused to lose.

WHEN REALITY HITS

Heaven

I was so pissed off arriving back to Ricardo's house. I had only gone into the office to grab something out my desk and let my boss know I needed more time off, but to be fired was something I was not expecting. I felt like she did it on purpose. She was not sympathetic or even concerned about why I needed the time. I mean she was not entitled to even care but when I first met her, she gave off the impression that she cared for her employees. I guess that was my dumb ass mistake. Getting out of the car and walking in the door to Ricardo's home that this nigga gave me a key to, I felt a comfort that I have been trying to avoid this whole time we have been messing around.

"Damn, why you walk in here so upset?" Ricardo asked me.

"My boss fired me. She didn't even ask me if I was ok," I was puzzled but more so offended and ashamed to be fired. I have never been fired from a job before.

"Well, what the hell made her do that?" Ricardo asked. I looked into his dreamy eyes, as he smoked the blunt that he held between his fingers.

"I mean I did tell her I needed additional time off, but the bitch was so uncaring and rude. I have never seen her to be that way. It threw me a little," I sat on the couch and propped my foot up in his lap. He grabbed my foot with his free hand and began to rub them. As I leaned my head back on the couch in distress. "I worked so hard for my career, and at her office in this short period of time. I'm just lost as to why she would easily let me go," I sighed deeply. I was becoming worn down about my job and this shit with Kia. I just wanted my cousin home and my dream job back. I was not meant or made to be a fucking hustler.

"Look, right now your cousin is way more important and should be your focus, and no I'm not saying you are wrong to still think about yourself. Just remember you can get another job. Let that bitch be flaw and keep it moving. Now if you want, I can definitely handle the situation." He tried to comfort me the best way he knew how to. No matter how ghetto the shit sounded. I smiled slightly because he was really rubbing me the right way at this point.

"No, I don't want you to do nothing to anyone sir," I laughed at the thought of him defending me. "But now I have to figure out work once this shit is over with once we get Kia back." I told him as I ran my fingers through my hair.

"Well, I got you, so don't stress yourself." he simply responded.

"Hmph, don't say that now…" I was cut off by the ringing of my phone. Lifting slightly to grab it. Seeing it was Caleb, I knew I needed to answer it. I moved my feet from his lap and stood up. "Let me take this call," I advised him, heading quickly towards the door. I struggled to quickly put my slides on and make it out the door. Once the door was closed. I was able to answer the phone before the call went to my voicemail.

"Hello," I sweetly answered.

"Heaven, why haven't you call me today?" Caleb demanded.

"Baby, I'm sorry I have been dealing with Kia and her being sick," I lied.

"Oh, so how she doing? What hospital you at?" he asked in a sarcastic tone. Removing my phone from my ear and looking at the phone trying to figure out what the fuck I was about to say as if me looking at the phone was going to provide the answers I needed to say on the screen. I knew this nigga must have popped up to the house or some shit. He was talking like he knew I wasn't there.

"She is doing much better. We're at Amber's house, we never went to a hospital," I let the lie roll off my tongue because I knew for sure the nigga didn't know where Amber stayed at.

"So, you stayed at Amber's house? That's weird being the fact all y'all cars was sitting in front of Kia's house but no one was home when I drove by last night to bring you food." His tone was dry, and I could tell he was pissed the hell off.

"Um, why would you just pop up and not call? Like that was dumb. You saw we were not there and didn't think to call my phone?" I tried to flip it back on him.

"Heaven, I'm not sure what you got going on, but you better bring your ass home tonight!" he snapped hanging up in my face. The fear I felt come over me made my ass panic. I walked back inside the house and went into the kitchen to take a breather without Ricardo looking at me.

"So yo nigga got you spooked," Ricardo's deep voice scared the hell out of me from behind. I never even heard him walk up on me.

"Listen, I can't do this anymore. I need to go." I turned around to face him. He stood tall over me. I could feel his body heat radiate all over. His breathing became heavy, as he stepped closer to me.

"So, you gon leave a nigga for that L seven ass nigga?" his face contorted in a mug that I was not feeling. What was I supposed to do or say? Ricardo knew that I had a man, but he was so adamant about fucking with me. Shit, I am not going to lie, it had its perks, but everything he did for me I could do for myself. I wasn't impressed or moved by his money, but I was amazed by his soul and the person he was. There was a side of him that most didn't see, but he allowed me to see very often.

"Look, you're making this harder than what it is. You knew what it was when we started." I simply put my head down because I couldn't look him in his brown eyes. I knew that looking at him would only get me to stay.

Looking back up our lips met, instantly as if he knew what he needed to do. The passion that erupted from the kiss had his hands roaming my body, making me slip light moans from my mouth. I leaned my head back as his mouth met my neck. The way his tongue and small suctions on my skin made chills go down my spine as I moan softly again. Just as I put my hands on his chest to push him back, he smoothly turned me around making me place my hands on the edge of the counter and wrapped his left hand around my neck and cupping my chin making me lean my head back as he passionately kissed me and slipped his hands down my tights to play with my flesh that was already dripping wet. As bad as I wanted him to stop, the way his touches, sucking and kisses had my mind on another planet. Don't get me wrong Caleb could fuck, but Ricardo knew how to make a bitch fall in love and dream about every encounter even while being wide awake. Before I could register what was going down, Ricardo had my tights down and my ass bent over on the counter pounding me steady and firm, with some aggression. I moaned every time he would push deep inside me hard. I was ready to explode, but he stopped and swiftly picked me up and took me to his room, where he yanked my clothes off and began licking me from the front to the back. The nigga was just nasty. I think I curled my toes so hard, I caught a cramp. He had my juices flowing like a running faucet. I was shaking trying to figure out why this man was making my body feel like this. Before I could take a deep breath after the orgasm he just gave me, he was pushing inside of me and covering my mouth with his that my damn juices was dripped in. He sucked on my tongue and gently bit and sucked on my bottom lip while he slowly grinded in me. I was just about to scream from another intense orgasm, but he covered my mouth with his and started pounding me in and out aggressively. I don't know what point he was trying to prove at the moment, but he was definitely letting me know he was the boss and ran shit. He flipped my body over and slowly went back inside me from the back and put all his weight on me, making me arch my back deep as he kept a steady pace. I swear Ricardo did this shit on purpose because that man knew I couldn't resist his ass. He made sure to work my body in overdrive until I was waking up with his body wrapped around me. Noticing the sun had gon down and it was nighttime, I began to panic. I eased my body from under him slowly and swiftly. I crept around the room grabbing my clothes and eased my way out of the room and down the hall to the guest bathroom. I quickly did a hoe a bath and put my clothes back on. I walked out of the bathroom and went to grab my purse, phone and keys. I had to see Caleb and talk to him. I wasn't sure what was about to happen, but I knew one thing, I couldn't stay in this house with Ricardo being confused as fuck. I sat his house key on the counter looked back towards the slightly open room door. Damn, this man was going to be mad I left, but I had a man at home, and this was a dangerous game we were playing especially when we are supposed to be working to find my cousin.

I left out of his house locking the bottom lock from the inside and I closed the door. I headed to my whip and cranked it up. I sat there for a few moments as tears began to fall down my eyes. For some reason I was too damn emotional, and the sad part for the first time ever the realization that Ricardo and I would be done, my feelings was completely hurt. I drove off and finally decided to look at my phone at the time and almost wanted to faint. The fact it was three am I knew Caleb was going to kill me. I noticed my miss calls from Amber and Mack. I decided to call Amber back.

"Hello," her voice sounded like a whole man being woken from out of his sleep.

"You called me?" I asked her.

"Yo Amber, whoever the fuck that is, hang that shit up. We got shit to handle in the am," I heard Mack snap in the background.

"Shut the fuck up its Heaven. I don't tell you nothing when your phone rings all night because of Tina's bitch ass!" Amber snapped, and then I heard shuffling of the phone for a few minutes before Amber came back on the phone. "Hey you ok? I was worried because Caleb's ass keeps calling me," Amber's voice was full of concern.

"Girl it's Ricardo. He is like a fucking love leech," I sighed in frustration.

"Bitch! Oh, my Gawd! You in love with that nigga!" she gasped at her own words.

"Amber, it's so crazy. I don't think that's it," I confessed. I wasn't sure what I felt but I knew it was a connection I never had before.

"Damn, well where are you? I'm not at Kia's. I'm at home, Mack's simple ass followed me home to find my shit. I know the feeling though of a love leech. Nigga just suck your love dry and make you crazy.

"Exactly, I'm heading home to Caleb, but I have an uneasy feeling." I finally was honest with myself and Amber.

"Listen, if the nigga gets froggy, call me. And honestly, I don't think you should go to him anyways. Like we already got Kia missing and shit. I definitely think you should just go home or come here." Amber was concerned and I could hear the doubt and worry in her voice.

"No, I need to reassure Caleb. That's all I have to do. Let him know there is no funny business going on. I can't keep up this shit with Ricardo." I truthfully told her.

"Honestly, Heaven, Ricardo is a better man for you regardless of his profession of choice, but I'm gon let you do you, because right now we have way more important shit to handle then your life.

Just don't die before we get Kia back." Amber seriously said.

"I'm going to be fine. I will see you tomorrow for the drop offs." I said before hanging up. Amber's words lingered in my head like a song on repeat. She was right about one thing. The bigger picture was helping my cousin.

I pulled into Caleb's driveway contemplating if I should get out or not. I wasn't scared but I did feel like he was going to blow his top. I grabbed my purse and got out the car. I began to fumble with the keys and before I could stick the key into the door, Caleb swung the door open aggressively. I jumped back from being startled.

"It's after three in the morning, I been calling your phone and you show up now like it's, ok?" His voice was so cold. I felt the chills come over me, making me shake. He stood tall over me, glaring, waiting for me to respond to what he had said. For the first time ever, I had lump in my throat. I felt like I couldn't speak or talk. Shit, if you ask me, I felt like I couldn't breathe.

"Listen…" I was cut off by his fist hitting my face. I was knocked flat on my ass. I grabbed my face feeling the wetness from my noise as I scurried back, trying not to get hit again. I couldn't scream from the shock. It felt like my face got hit by a hammer the way it throbbed as I held it. I tried to reach for my key chain so I could get to the pepper spray, but he kicked it out of the way and then grabbed me by my hair and dragged me in the house. I couldn't yell. I couldn't do shit. I was stunned because Caleb promised me no matter what this part of him had died.

"Bitch, did you know your stupid ass had hickeys all over your fucking neck! Lying and shit and you out here being a fucking hoe!" I felt Caleb rip my shirt open and his face looked as if the devil himself went and possessed his body. I could kick myself for not looking in the mirror in the bathroom. I didn't even pay attention to any marks because I just needed to wash my pussy and dip out. He dragged me to the bathroom and flip the switch. My neck was definitely marked up, as well as my breast and the sides of my stomach. I had sucking and bite marks all over my light skin. This nigga did it in places that was very much visible. I never even notice them because I was so in a rush to leave his house. The way Caleb starred at me in pure disgust, I knew he was going to attack me again. I watched the murderous look in his eyes and took running for the front door. Before I could make it out the door, he knocked my stupid ass unconscious. I guess next time I will listen to Amber.

A FIGHT FOR MY LIFE

Kia

I opened my eyes realizing I fell asleep after listening to Nadia and the nurse talk. I knew from the conversation they had, that I had a chance now to try and get this lock off my feet. One thing for sure I could pick a damn lock. That was something I learned as a little girl. I used to love to play with locks and my grandmother hated it. I didn't know today it would benefit me so much, since it was something that would get me cursed out on a daily by my grandmother. I grabbed a section of the blanket and used my teeth to rip a piece of it to use to wrap around my arm once I pulled the IV line out. I gently pulled the IV line out of my arm and tied the sheet around my arm tight using it as a band-aide. I quickly got up and grabbed the needle from under my pillow that I was able to sneak from the nurse, and my made shift Bobby pin from the bed spring I was able to create during the times I was left alone. I began to try and fumble with the lock on my leg. I struggled for a while. I started to feel pain in my side, and I began to rub my stomach slowly in the area of the pain. I was trying to keep myself calm, but my anxiousness was getting the best of me. I was getting too excited, and I don't think it was good for the baby the way I was starting to feel the sharp pains. Once the pain subsided, I tried again at the lock. After what felt like hours the lock made a click sound and to see the lock open and release, I wanted to cry. I was finally free and just needed to get the fuck out the door. I pulled the chain from around my ankle and slowly got up. I felt the pressure pushing down on my pelvic and I felt like soon this baby was going to come. I held my stomach as I tried to move towards the door. The sound of keys at a lock made me wobble quickly back into the bed covering the open lock with the blanket as well as my leg. I wasn't sure who was coming inside but I knew I needed to fight my way out. Seeing Nadia round the corner made my heartbeat speed up. She was looking down at her phone making this the perfect moment to surprise her ass really good. As I quickly thought of what to do, she finally looked up at me.

"Oh, you're awake good because…!" her words got caught in her mouth as she looked at me and then at the IV bag that was no longer attached to and then back at me. I could kick myself for, forgetting to move the IV bag close to me so she wouldn't notice. At that moment I knew I didn't have time to think it was all reaction. She went to reach in her back, but the way I hopped up and landed a quick jab to her nose making the crimson red liquid flow down her nose instantly. She stumbled back grabbing her face from the shock of being caught off guard and I took another two jabs to her face with my fist aiming at her eyes. She at that point fell back hitting the wall hard. I tried to kick her as hard as I could in her stomach, and then I gave her another kick to her face quickly knocking her to the floor flat. She looked unconscious and I immediately ran towards the stairs but the pains in my stomach was causing me to move slowly up the stairs. I felt her hand wrap around my leg as she tried to pull me down. With the pain I was feeling I tried to shake her away from my leg, but I gave out after one sharp pain hit my side, allowing her to yank me down hard causing me to fall on my knees. I yelled out in pain. As I turned over as my stomach began to cramp up hard. This baby was truly the seed of chuckie the way it was balling up, making my stomach cramp. Trying to breathe through all the pain I was feeling in my body, Nadia tried to pull me down again, but with all the strength I could muster up, I kicked her hard in the face with my free leg making her fall back hitting her head. I could tell she was dazed because she slowly moved her head from side to side. She looked like she could barely move, or something was broken in her body.

I took a deep breath and continued up the stairs to the door. I was able to open it and free myself from the hell I been in. I noticed I was in Vinny's office, and I tried my best to move quickly to the other door that would lead me out of his office and to the hallway of the house. I turned the knob to the door opening it letting the fresh air hit my face. I tried quickly to move down the hall, towards the front door. I looked back and since I didn't see her. I continued moving down the hall and I winced in pain with every step I took. I was determined to save my baby's life. I was rounding the corner to make it to the front door, but I felt something hit me hard in the back of my head making me hit the floor. The pain was worse than my stomach. I was barely conscious, but I could hear screaming, yelling and tussling. I felt someone pick me up right before everything went black.

Hearing a heart monitor and beeping sounds my eyes slowly opened and then closed. They felt heavy. I began to move my arms and legs. I then took my right hand and placed it on my stomach and my baby begin to move. I sighed in relief at knowing he or she was still ok. I finally opened my eyes and felt a hand in my left hand. I turned my head in that direction and I never felt so good to see the Jet-black waves. I squeezed his hand, and he looked up and when our eyes met, he jumped up and for the first time ever I seen tears form and fall down his eyes. He began kissing my forehead and cheeks.

"Shit man, a nigga never been so scared in my life," he expressed "I'm so sorry shawty. A nigga is fucked up behind this shit," he continued.

"I'm just…" I tried to clear my dry throat.

"Listen, let me call the nurse and get you some ice." He said but I held on to his hand tight.

"Please, don't leave me please," I began to panic. I was afraid to be alone. The last time I was alone I was snatched by a crazy bitch.

"Ok, ok let me just push the nurse button, so someone can come check you while you up." He said never letting my hand go. He reached across me doing exactly that. At this point I was paranoid. I didn't feel comfortable being alone especially with me being pregnant. The door swung open, and the nurse came in. She was older black woman. She smiled pleasantly.

"How are you feeling?" she asked.

"Her throat is dry," Renzo answered for me.

"No problem, I'm going to check your vitals and then I have two police officers outside ready to ask questions." She advised. She seemed a little skeptical of Renzo, but little did she know it was not him that harmed me. I had every intention on blaming the attack on a woman. If I had it my way, the bitch that had me suffering would be dead or I would press charges and make her prissy ass do time, but because of what we did to make money, I didn't want any problems with the police. The nurse checked my vitals and then checked the back of my head and the bandage.

"Listen, everything seems good. Your baby is strong, and it seems like the baby was able endure the attack that happened to you. I hope you are better and safe now." She said side eyeing Renzo.

"The fuck you looking at me for? I didn't do this shit!" he snapped on the nurse. I squeezed his hand so he could calm down. He turned and looked at me and the wrinkles on his forehead disappeared and he softened his look at me.

"I will be back with your ice chips and cold water," The nurse said without even looking at Renzo. She was now a little nervous and quickly passed him to walk back out the door. After about five minutes, she was back with the water and ice chips. Renzo grabbed the water and took his time giving me sips to quench my thirst. The police officers walked in.

"Hello Ms. Grey, I'm Detective Gibson and this is my partner Detective Shaw. We are here to ask a few questions regarding your attack. Do you know who would attack you?" he asked.

"It was a woman. I don't know her, and I can barely remember how it happened." I said giving them all the details that they would get out of me.

"Where the attack take place?" he asked, and I got even more annoyed.

"Look I don't remember, I did get hit in the head. I just remembered it being a woman because of her voice, other than that I don't remember," I shut down any further questioning they thought they were going to do.

"Listen, if you can remember anything please contact us," The officer sighed as if I was another domestic dispute about to go wrong. He handed me a card and walked out with his partner right behind them.

"I see you still the same person." Renzo smirked, but I couldn't smile nor laugh.

"No, I'm not. I'm afraid Renzo as hard and as strong as I am, I'm fucking scared and the bitch that did this to me was someone you were dealing with who couldn't handle the fact you really was never going to leave me alone?" I said as the tears flowed down. I felt dumb for even feeling like I needed Renzo. He was the reason I was in this situation, with a bruised head, pregnant and in bad health. He was the root of all my damn problems.

"Listen, Lolita and I are going to find her, and a nigga promises she won't touch you again." He tried to reassure me.

"The fuck you mean you will find her? Where the fuck did she go? She hit me in the back of the head. The bitch kidnapped me" I raised my voice. My monitors started going off like crazy, bringing the nurse in.

"Listen Ms. Grey you must stay calm as possible. Your child needs not to go in distress. We already had to stop you from going into labor multiple times." She expressed and I looked at her with confusion.

"You almost lost the baby, and they have been trying to keep the baby in as long as possible." Renzo answered the question I was just about to ask.

"Exactly, so we need you not to get worked up to keep the baby in and healthy," She smiled, as she adjusted the monitors on my stomach to get a strong sound of the heartbeat of the baby. Soon as she walked out. I turned to Renzo.

"I know Kia, I promise. I will find her," he pleaded for me to trust his word.

"Oh, I know because you better dead this shit or else." I finally said before the room door swung open and in walked in the whole gang. Amber ran towards me planting kisses on me, right behind my mom and aunts. Chase, Mack and Ricardo brought in flowers and balloons and gifts. I faintly smiled. I was happy to see them, but I was physically and mentally drained.

"Oh my God, are you ok? Why is this bandage on your head? Is the baby ok?" Amber asked question after question. I was happy to see them, but my spirit was disturbed because this crazy bitch was still free. I watched Renzo try to move away from me, but I held his hand tight. The last time he left, I almost died. I don't think I was comfortable yet even with people around. He stared at me and gave me a look of reassurance that he wasn't leaving.

"Please say something," Amber looked at me with tears in her eyes. I knew they were tears of joy because she was so happy to see me.

"Amber, I don't want to talk about it," I honestly told her. She nodded her head in understanding and just sat next to me and grabbed my hand. I looked around the room as all the guys huddled together talking. I looked around again realizing Heaven was not here. "Amber, where is Heaven?" I asked. I was becoming so exhausted suddenly. I yawned big, as my baby began to stir around in my stomach.

"Um, that's a good question. I called her multiple times and left multiple messages, but she hasn't responded yet. Let me call her again," she said getting up to go call her again. I watched Renzo walk back over to me and sit down in the chair beside me. He grabbed my hand and held it firmly, while he placed his other hand on my stomach.

"You ok?" he asked. I nodded my head yes, but honestly, I wasn't. I hated being helpless. I felt helpless because a bitch was able to get close to me, and honestly in the condition I was in there was nothing I could do about it.

"Damn, Ric you spoke to Heaven?" Amber asked.

"Um, naw she left my house in the middle of the night to go back to that nigga, and I haven't heard from her since," he truthfully spoke. I think was the only one shock that he even said she was at his house. Last time I knew they were fucking, but she was adamant that was all they will be doing.

"Um, Ric can you go with me outside let me talk to you?" Amber said, but I wanted to know what the hell was going on and why Heaven wasn't here. I prayed that nothing bad happened to Heaven, because I don't think I could handle any bad news. I knew something was wrong with me because I didn't have the energy to do anything not even eat. Hearing my stomach rumble for the first-time alarmed Renzo, he sat back in the chair quickly.

"When the last time you ate?" he asked worried.

"Not sure, but I'm exhausted, and I want to leave here," I honestly spoke. I did not feel safe. I wanted to always be around a damn gun, but with me being in the hospital that just wasn't possible.

"You want to go home?" he asked, and I shook my head no looking at that nigga as if he was crazy. He already knew at that point I wanted somewhere new and safe. I was not about to stay somewhere that was easy access to that psycho bitch of his.

"Just make sure Heaven is ok first, then get me out of here." I expressed. He stared at me and nodded his head in agreement. I laid my head back as my eyes became heavy like weights. I knew I was sleepy, and I think since I had everyone here with me, it's like my mind and body knew it could finally rest a little. When the darkness came over me, I said a silent prayer for my cousin.

WRONG MOVE

Amber

I stood in the hall of the hospital with Ricardo and Renzo, trying to figure out where the hell Heaven was. I was worried at this point and if that bitch ass nigga Caleb did something to her, I was going to shoot his ass. Ricardo tried her cell, but he went straight to voicemail. At that point we knew he was on block. I tried again multiple times and nothing. I finally got one of my cousins back, but now the other one is missing.

"You don't know where the nigga lives?'"' Ricardo asked me.

"No, I don't. She just started back talking to the stupid nigga and honestly knowing Heaven she probably been messing with the nigga for a while now. She is really good at keeping her personal shit a secret and telling everyone else shit." I got annoyed thinking about how shady her ass could be at times.

"Well, what did she say the last time you talked to her?" Ricardo asked me, and I began to think about Heaven and I's last conversation.

"Well, she said she was leaving you and headed to Caleb's house since he had been blowing up her phone. She did seem scared, and I told her not go, and to just come home to my house, but she refused. She basically said she wanted to go to Caleb's before he got even more upset."

"Well, it shouldn't be hard to find out where this nigga lives. Have Chase get you an address, and Amber calm down. I'm sure she is ok." Renzo tried to be positive, but something in my gut was telling me that something was terribly wrong. I knew my cousin. She wouldn't dare not answer her phone for this long.

"How long you think it will take Chase to find out?" The worry on my face was evident. I stood back and looked at an already tired Renzo. I had to admit, he really did step up to the plate when it came to my cousin. He tried his best to figure it out, but I always knew if he wouldn't save her, my cousin would save herself. She was a strong person, and I never knew her to back down from any challenge brought her way.

"Look, Chase and I will find her. Do you at least know where the nigga works?" he asked me and honestly, I couldn't remember the name, but I sure did remember how to get there.

"Not sure of the name of the place, but I damn sure can show or tell you how to get there." I assured them.

"That will work. Tell Ricardo how to get there. I'm going to get Chase now and tell him to slide," Renzo stated before he walked back into Kia's hospital room.

"Damn, you think something happen?" A worried look crept on my face, as Ricardo stared down at me and placed me in a brotherly hug.

"Look just chill. She going to be alright and if she not, trust I'm gon take action behind shawty." He advised. I nodded my head in understanding. Renzo came back out the room with Mack and

Chase. They looked like they were about to be on go.

"Renzo put me up on game. I'm good with directions, Amber. Tell me how to get there," he asked. I broke down how to get to Caleb's job in the easiest way I knew how to Chase, before him and Ricardo left. My nerves were shot. I had finally felt good for a little bit, when we got the call about Kia, but now I was on edge because of Heaven.

"You coming back in?" Renzo asked me. I honestly didn't want to walk in without Heaven next to me. I didn't want to worry Kia. She already been through so much. Her last and finally moments of her pregnancy needed to be filled with some type of happiness.

"Umm, no I don't want to come in without Heaven. I'm going to leave and get some from fresh air." I told him. He nodded his head in understanding.

"I'm going to stay with Amber," Mack said.

"No, you stay with Renzo. I need some space. I need to be alone," I told him. Mack looked at me as if I was crazy.

"The fuck you talkin about alone? I'm not leaving you to go be alone." He raised his voice.

"Listen, I just need some space to breathe. Why are you smothering me?" I snapped.

"I'm going inside. I'm gon let y'all fight that out," Renzo said, before going back in the room with Kia.

"A nigga not smothering you. You trying to get your ass back to that damn nigga." He looked at me with disgust.

"Nigga, please. Both of you could kiss my little ass, because I have way more things to think about then a nigga. Like what is wrong with you. I got one cousin back now the other one is missing," I rolled my eyes, because the sight of him was enough to make me cringe.

"We know where Heaven is. Let's be honest she laid up with that damn nigga or he beat her ass into a coma. Heaven should have left that nigga alone," Mack was clearly irritated about Heaven going back to Caleb. We all knew what he did to her before.

"Look, I will see y'all later. I can't deal with all this shit," I said and began to walk off. I knew Mack was mad and burning a hole into me, but I didn't care I needed to go clear my damn head.

Making into my car, I drove off and headed south on the I-95 expressway. I didn't have a particular destination I was headed to, but I continued to drive so I could think. I was trying so hard to figure out why were all these bad things happening to my family. I knew one common denominator and that was fucking men. Everything that happened to Kia, was behind a nigga. Everything that happened to Heaven was behind a nigga, well and her own stupid decisions as well. I wondered to myself would I be next? Would my downfall be behind a nigga? I just knew whatever I did, I needed to make sure that I was clear to both men in my life so that they had an exceptionally good understanding of how shit was about to flow around me. I refused to end up like my damn cousins. Lost in the damn sauce of a man. I felt like right now that's what it was with me and Mack. I was so blinded by loving him, I wasn't choosing myself. I somehow found myself at Troy's place. I contemplated going to the door for about ten minutes. I sat wondering if I was really doing the right thing. I got out the car and made my way to the door. I knocked on the door and patiently waited for him to answer. After a few minutes I could hear the locks turning at the door and then I laid eyes on his handsome face.

"Damn, what do I owe the visit? I thought it was all business from here on out."

"I need to talk to you," I truthfully answered. He nodded his head and moved aside on the crutches to let me in. He closed and locked the door as he made his way to his favorite spot on the couch. I sat down next to him, and he stared at me, making me slightly uncomfortable.

"We found Kia, and now Heaven is missing," I finally spoke.

"Yea, I heard. One of yo man's peoples told me. We still moving the dope though, so why you here?" he asked.

"I needed to talk to someone and you're the only person I can talk to without feeling like I'm about to lose it," I honestly said, finally letting shaking my sandals off my feet and pulling my legs up on the couch further, getting comfortable.

"Look, no offense Amber, I can't be your friend. It's hard enough I'm working with your boy for a little and now I got to watch y'all two interact just to see some get back on my nigga's name. Man, I don't know that's some hard shit, especially when a nigga got crazy feelings for you." He truthfully told me.

"Troy, how would we ever be like that when I have to see this nigga all the time since we own a business together? Like I'm real life a business owner of a successful company. Why would I want to give up something that I worked so hard for? You know with us trying a relationship, I would have to not be in business with Mack and that is not happening. I worked to damn hard… but honestly, I can't lose you as a friend. You are a damn good person, until you're mad and ready to kill me," I rolled my eyes at the last part. Troy stared at me for a few moments and sighed deeply.

"Man, I guess we will figure this shit out, but Amber if we are friends, that's what it will be. Ain't no fucking or none of that shit. A nigga got feelings too." He expressed. I wasn't feeling it, but it will do for now.

"Alright, that's fair," I said and readjusted myself on the couch. My phone began to ring taking me out my thoughts. Seeing it was Heaven's number I jumped up immediately and answered the phone.

"Hello, Heaven? Are you ok? Hello Heaven?" I kept saying into the phone, but I barely could hear her.

"Help me," I heard her faint voice say. I began to panic.

"Heaven, where are you? Can you tell me?"
I asked her. I heard shuffling of the phone and it
sounded like she was trying to text.

"Is everything ok?" Troy curiously asked. I
put my index finger to my lips to "shh" him.

"Listen Heaven please tell me where you
are. Can you share your location?" I asked her
again, but the line was quiet. The phone made the
noise of a lost signal and hung up. I was going to
call back, but I went to my text messages. I was
about to send her a message just in case the crazy
nigga walked in or something, but then I noticed she
shared her location. My adrenaline began to pump
through my veins. I slipped on my slides quickly
and grabbed my purse.

"What's going on?" Troy asked alarmed.

"Heaven is missing, and she finally made
contact and shared her location. I just need to hurry
up to the location before it stops being shared." I
quickly rushed to the door.

"You want me to go with you?" he asked but honestly, I didn't want him to get hurt. He definitely wasn't 100% and couldn't do shit to help.

"I will be ok. I'll call you once I find out what's going on," I advised him. He nodded his head agreement before I rushed out the door. Soon as my butt touch the car seat, I began dialing Ricardo. I cranked the car up and put the phone on speaker so I could pull up the shared location. I began to drive towards the location, so that I could try and make it to my cousin.

"Yo," Ricardo came through the speaker of the phone.

"Ric, Heaven called me. She could barely talk." I began to get emotional.

"Amber, calm down and talk." Ricardo coaxed. I cleared my throat and wiped my eyes, as I looked down at the map to be sure I was going the right way.

"She shared her location, I will share mine with you so you can follow me, but it looks like I'm

151

heading west on pines towards the 75," I said to him.

"Aiight, bet. Listen do not knock on the door or do anything until we get there," He informed me.

"Ok," I said but I was too antsy. I could barely stop shaking. I was a nervous wreck and eager to get to the bottom of what the hell was going on. I continued my drive until I made it to the destination on the GPS. I parked down some from the home but made sure it was in my eyesight. I sat and looked around the neighborhood and I had to admit it was nice. My eyes went back to the house. It seemed dark inside like no one was home. I couldn't wait anymore. I grabbed my purse that held my gun in it. I cocked the gun back and held it in my hand inside the bag, while I quickly got out the car and ran across the street towards the home that showed Heaven was in as swiftly as possible. I double checked my surroundings, and the street was quiet and empty, which was really weird to me. When I walked quickly up to the door, I peeped in the window, and I didn't see anyone. It was dark in the house. I went around the back of the home, to try and see if they had any back windows. I finally made it to the back yard where the glass doors gave me a full view of the bottom of the house. The fact I saw smeared blood on the floor my heart broke. Trying to get my emotions in check, I grabbed the door handle to try and turn it but it was locked. I started to look around the house and on the floor for a rock, but I noticed the window was slightly ajar by the kitchen. I moved quickly to get the screen off, but it was hard. I looked in my purse for my keys that held a pocketknife and pepper spray. Say what you want, but we lived in the worst times. I needed everything in case I couldn't get to my gun. I began to cut in the screen, and I pushed against the window glass and began to push it up. I finally got the window to where I could climb inside. Once I was inside, I took my gun out pointing it. I moved swiftly through the house as I followed the smeared blood trails on the floor. I opened one door to my right, and it was the bathroom that had blood on the floor and in the sink. I walked back out and continued down the hall with my gun pointed. I could hear slight moans further down the hall. I continued toward the noises. When I made it to the room, I pushed the door open with my gun still drawn in front of me. I found Heaven on the floor in the corner moaning in pain. My eyes watered at the sight before me. I ran towards her, scared to touch her because I might hurt her. I moved her carefully as her body jerked away scared.

"Heaven, it's me, it's Amber." I touched her again, and she began crying. I put the gun down and grabbed my cell phone out of my purse. I dialed Ricardo.

"Ric, she is here. Hurry she is fucked up, and I don't think he is here," I quickly said into the phone as soon as he answered.

"Just sit tight the GPS says we three minutes away," He confirmed.

"Ok, please hurry. She looks bad," I expressed, before hanging up. I got up and made my way to the adjoining bathroom. I grabbed some towels and we them. I walked back out and began to gently wipe her face. I wanted to cry so bad because her lip and eye was swollen. I swear she had to have some broken bones, but I knew Heaven would not want to go to the hospital. She was embarrassed and I could see it in her face as she cried.

"Heaven, can you talk?" I asked her and she nodded her head. "Can you walk?" she nodded her head no. "Listen, Heaven talk to me please. Where is Caleb?" I asked.

"It hurts too much to talk," she began breathing hard.

"Ok, just stay calm. Let me just clean your face a little," I told her and dabbed her face with the wet towel. My phone vibrated and seeing it was Ricardo I answered.

"We at the front door," Ricardo said, and I got up and ran towards the door and unlocked it. Soon as I open the door, Ricardo and Chase rushed inside and followed behind me. I guided them to the room where Heaven was laid up in.

"Shit, the fuck," Chase said at the sight of Heaven. She looked extremely bad because she had blood all over her. We wouldn't know really what happened until we get her somewhere to see. Her eyes were purple and blue, she had knots on the top of her head, blood was dried up around her nose and mouth. She her wrist and hands had blood on them. I wanted to cry so bad because this exactly how she looked but worst last time. This time it's like he spared her ass. I was so fucking mad and sad at the same time, I didn't know what to do with myself.

"Man, just help me get her out of here before this nigga shows up and I go to fucking jail for murder too fucking early," Ricardo choked. I could tell the sight of her was eating him alive. They began to lift her off the floor and she moaned loudly in pain. I just knew this gurl had to have something broken. I searched for her purse and saw it tossed on a chair. I dug in it to be sure her keys and phone was inside. Once I realized it was there, I followed behind Chase and Ricardo who was carrying Heaven outside. We quickly got her in my truck with Ricardo holding her like a baby. Chase closed the door and I hopped in the driver seat of my truck and turned the car on.

"Let's get her to a hospital," Chase said.

"Nooo, please no," Heaven yelled out. She sounded like she was in agony. I was mad and confused. The hell she means no don't take her to the hospital. I turned my head towards the back, and I could tell Ricardo was getting upset, and torn between leaving her ass and caring for her.

"The fuck you talking about no? This nigga got you out here looking crazy, and you don't want to go to the ER? Girl you could have broken bones." I expressed clearly annoyed.

"Noo, noo please," Is all she could reply.

"Just drive to my house. Chase knows a nurse. I will have him hit shawty up to come through," Ricardo stated visibly annoyed, but more so concerned. Shaking my head, I turned around and drove off. I knew once Caleb realized she was gone, he was going to panic like crazy. This nigga has lost all of his brain functions to think doing this was ok and we wouldn't catch up to his ass. I drove towards Ricardo house thinking about my cousins and their different situations. Shit, honestly, I thought out of all of us that Heaven had the most common sense when it came to a man. Now, I see she just as stupid as us. Seeing these both go through something crazy made me realize as much as I loved Mack, I was not about to put up with shit that was going to cause my sanity, and yea I liked Troy, but there was no way I was dealing with his sensitive ass either. They were both good men with different qualities. I just couldn't handle the drama they both will bring. I rather be alone or find a whole new man at this point. This was too much, and I was not about to be the next person in some crazy shit. I finally pulled up to Ricardo's house. I jumped out the truck as he got out and slowly picked Heaven up. I closed the back seat door and hurriedly followed behind him to the door. He struggled trying to turn the keys around to get to the right key.

"Nigga, just ask for help damn," I snatched the keys. "Which one?" I questioned.

"It's the only silver key on the key ring," He stated. Selecting the only silver key on the ring, I inserted the key in the door. Turning it to unlock the door. I pushed the door in and held it open for him to come in. I closed the door and locked it. I watched him carry Heaven to the couch.

"Heaven baby, talk to me," his voice held so much concern. He spoke gentle to her and caressed her arm. She was fucked up, but I thank God it wasn't as bad as the last time.

"Amber stay right here. Let me go get towels and shit," he told me as he got up. His face was distorted, and he began to look angry and frustrated.

"He's mad," Her voice was above a whisper. I got closer to her and rubbed her hair,

"Shhh. He will be fine. I need you to get better. Heaven you need to go to the hospital," I pleaded.

"No," she shook her head slowly. I could tell she was in pain. She was scared to barely move. Ricardo walked back in with towels, a bowl and a first aid kit. This nigga was too prepared if you asked me. He sat next to Heaven and stared at her. She put her head down in embarrassment. He began to wet the cloth and gently clean the blood off her face. She winced in pain with every touch. I got mad all over again and left out of the living room. I walked past the dining room and kitchen, admiring the décor of the home. I could tell he had an interior decorator come in and decorate his home. It didn't have a regular woman's touch it had skilled touch. The blended blues and oranges gave masculinity with a little softness. The kitchen was open and spacious. I know Heaven would love to cook in this kitchen. I was just about to walk my nosey self down the hall when someone ring the doorbell.

"I got it!" I yelled out heading towards the door. I knew it was Chase since he had to bring the nurse back. Opening the door and seeing the face of a pretty woman, took me back. I then saw Chase walking up behind her.

"Hi, come in," I said moving out of the way so they could walk inside.

"How is she doing?" Chase said to me as soon I closed the door.

"Not good. She is being stubborn," I truthfully told him. "She refuses to go to the hospital," I continued.

"Aiight, well this Keema. She is going to look at her for us," Chase introduces the nurse.

"Hello, can I take a look at her?" She asked, and I nodded my head yes. I noticed she had a whole bag that must be held medical supplies. She followed behind me and when she saw Heaven, I knew from the look she gave she wanted to ask what the hell happened, but she decided against it. She got close and open her bag and began to tend to Heaven. Ricardo stepped out the living room, with Chase and I right behind him. We all had a look of disgust. This shit with our circle was getting out of hand.

"So, what a nigga supposed to sit here and take care of her ass looking like this and shit? She don't want to go to the hospital and I can guarantee she gon be mad if I put a hot one in the nigga for trying her. So, what's a nigga supposed to do?" He pleaded with me and Chase. We were at a loss of words because honestly, we agreed with Him. I told her not to go over there, but she wouldn't listen because she has this stupid notion about a street nigga.

"If you want she can come home with me, and I will take care of her," I offered. He looked at me and I could tell he was in deep thought.

"You can stay here and take care of her," He advise.

"What? Why?" I frowned my face in aggravation.

"Look, the nigga knows where y'all stay at, and I don't want shit popping off while we gone," Ricardo stated.

"Nigga you not the only one with a pistol, the hell. I need my space from y'all niggas," My aggravation levels were at an all-time high.

"Nigga, I don't care what you do. You and Mack not together and it ain't my duty to keep tabs on yo pussy. I need you to take care of Heaven where I can be sure she is fucking safe." Ricardo snapped and walked out the door and made sure he slammed it. Chase looked at me and shook his head.

"Amber, shit ain't always about a nigga keeping tabs. Right now, it's about y'all safety. Renzo and Heaven have created an unsafe environment for all of y'all, so being careful is way more important, and say what you want Mack has tabs on your pussy even when you think he don't, so don't be no fool," He chuckled and walked in the kitchen. I followed behind him.

"The hell you mean he got tabs on me?" I asked Chase, wanting to know what the hell he knew.

"C'mon now, you think for one second Mack gon let you be happy with someone else? The nigga like your sneaky pussy ass. Shit, if I was him, I would have let the streets have you, but it's something about you that makes the nigga come back every damn time. He's dumb as fuck if you ask me," he truthfully spoke.

"So, you think I ain't shit?" I curiously asked Chase.

"Nah, you're not honest and that's fucking scary. No nigga wants a lying ass broad. You sneaky too, which makes it even worse. I could never fuck with someone like you. Now, as a friend you hold that shit down, which is mad weird. Maybe you letting a nigga change your true character and honestly speaking, if I change a woman for being her true self, I don't want her because that shit there is fucking dangerous." Chase dropped some knowledge on me. As young as he was, he was truly the definition of a real nigga in my book. He walked away and back into the living room with Heaven. He left me to my thoughts. Chase was the one that always spoke facts and he did have a point. I let Mack change me. I was so blinded by love I was willing to do what I had to do to keep it. Now, that shit right there was dangerous. So, Chase's logic was definitely true. I needed to get back to myself and learn myself all over again before I could ever love properly.

"Hey, your cousin is ok. I did not see or feel any broken bones, but again I don't have an x-ray in front of me to confirm that. She is swollen, but if you notice the swelling doesn't start to go down after a week, please take her to a hospital. She has lots of bruising to her body. It's going to hurt for her to walk on her right leg so be careful with moving her from place to place. I would say ice her down for the swelling and inflammation. I gave her some pain medication and left some for you to give to her as needed. Please, watch her overnight to be sure she is ok because she banged her head pretty bad. I have stitched her up in the back of the head, and on the side of her eyebrow. It may leave a scar depending on how her skin heals. If you need anything just call me," Keema came in and gave me the run down on what was wrong with Heaven. I thanked God it wasn't bad like last time. I took Keema's card.

"Aigght, holla if you need me Ambs," Chase said and put his hand in the small of Keema's back and guiding her out the door. I went back in the living room and shook my head at the site of Heaven.

"Heaven, let's get you in the tub so I can clean you up and rub you down so you can rest," I said to her, and she looked at me so pitiful. I looked at her and tried to show empathy, but to be honest I was plain mad, because I got stuck taking care of her after I told her ass to not go to the niggas house.

FAMILY TIES

Renzo

I sat in the chair speaking with Lolita. It had been a whole month since we got Kia back and Nadia went missing. When we found her, I walked in on Crown helping Kia up and Nadia had already fled the scene. To be honest, I don't think she fled. I think Lolita and her father are hiding her crazy ass. Lolita was doing the count from the dope that Nadia stole. I sat silently while Crown stood beside her. It's funny how Lolita became in charge and was fully running the show. She glanced up at me and smiled. Her beauty would always put the best to shame. This woman could hold a marathon with the youngest at her age.

"Renzo, thank you for not cutting ties with us due to the mishap. I will cover all Kia's medical expenses if need be. I will also let you keep all your earnings since you returned the rest of the dope Nadia stole. That is my gift to you since my husband couldn't keep his niece under control. I also assure you, you will not have any problems because I have tracked her down and she will be handled accordingly." She continued to write down things in her notepad. I wasn't honestly trying to hear all that. I wanted to deal with her my way, and a part of me felt like this shit would never be done. Nadia was obsessed with being with me and the fact she feels like Kia is the problem, I don't think she will stop when it comes to getting rid of Kia. This whole she will be handled was definitely not sitting well with me.

"Renzo, I can see the doubt," She finally stopped writing and stared into my eyes.

"I mean let's be for real. She wants Kia dead. You really think she will stop?" I asked Lolita. I was definitely filled with doubt.

"Renzo, trust when I say she won't be able to reach you or your family and that's my word. You need to make sure your focus is on Kia. Making sure she has a healthy baby and ready to get back to herself." She offered her reassurance and advice. Honestly, I wasn't feeling it, but I had to keep it real with myself. Lolita never did no snake shit nor did her husband Vinny. I just had to trust they would keep that nut job of niece the fuck away from me and my family.

"Listen, Lolita if she comes near us, I'm letting you know in advance, I'm going to be a real nigga first and she going to be eating a bullet. That shit she did was crazy as fuck, and I don't got time for no extra shit with her ass." I truthfully informed her.

"That's only fair, since your family dealt with a lot. Now down to business, I'm going to get your next shipment together for next month, but I know you normally get a mixture of drugs, weed and pills, right?" she questioned.

"Yea, but I'm going to have you in touch with Mack. I need to sit down for a while and help Kia." I advised her. She nodded her head in agreement.

"Well, then I understand. We are done here, and I have a gift for the baby," she stood and smiled.

"You didn't have to Lolita," I told her as I stood up from my chair.

"I know, but I wanted to," she responded and walked out of the office, and I followed behind her, with Crown behind me. I followed her inside the huge living room. There was a whole stroller car seat and hand carry bassinet by Bugaboo. I only knew the brand because Kia kept telling me to buy it, but I just didn't see myself spending all that money for a damn car seat and a stroller. Her ass wasn't going walking nowhere and the Target car seats look good to me.

"Damn, this shit dope. Thanks Lolita," I admired the box that held the travel system in it. It was a nice gift, but I was sure it was another peace offering for the shit we went through.

"Glad you like it. Crown can you put this in the car for him, and next time we meet, hopefully we can see that beautiful baby of yours." Lolita smiled as she embraced me. I'm not going to lie, shit felt weird. Something just felt off and I no longer trusted them. I knew for sure it wasn't them that held Kia hostage, but I did believe they were sweeping the shit under the rug because it was Vinny's crazy ass niece that did the shit. Crown did his best trying to fit the big box inside the whip. I said my goodbyes and drove farther away from the house. I immediately called Mack, so I could tell him what happened.

"Yo," Mack came through the line. I could hear Amber fussing in the background and knew immediately I called at the wrong time.

"Man, the hell you got going on? Ain't she supposed to be with Heaven?" I asked. It had been also a month since Heaven was attacked and we have been keeping her under close watch since her ass didn't want us to handle the nigga.

"Man, she took a break from Heaven's retarded ass, but she over here mad because Tina dropped my daughter off and knows where she lives," He sounded aggravated about the situation.

"Well, why the hell would you tell her where Amber lives?" I thought that was the dumbest shit ever.

"I didn't. The silly ass girl had to follow me one day. The bitch got mad because I told her I wasn't watching Maliyah anymore if she don't dump that baby in her stomach. Her ass got mad, and I guess she decided to follow me to Amber's house since I have not been home. Silly ass girl dropped my damn daughter off on the doorstep and hauled ass. Now, Amber is going crazy and won't shut the fuck up," He was definitely aggravated and annoyed. His tone of his voice told it all. Next thing I knew it sounded like the phone took a tumble and then I heard Amber's crazy ass in the background.

"Next time I'm going to break that shit! I told you to let me stomp the baby out the bitch, but no your ass wants to still play house with her! You know what, I'm gone," Amber yelled in the background. I could hear Mack yelling out back to Amber as it sounded like he was fumbling with the phone at the same time. After a few more words I heard the door slam.

"Man, this fucking girl has lost her damn mind," Mack stated.

"Mack, just make the damn girl get rid of the baby. The fuck so hard about that shit," I was confused why he still had Tina running around with a baby in her stomach and shit.

"Because nigga, it's her body and I can't make the girl do shit. Clearly she doesn't give a fuck. I ain't got too much of a choice," he sounded defeated. I knew he loved Amber, because it was no way in hell I would have ever let that bitch come back after the shit she pulled with me and Tina. Then had the nerve to be talking to the opp. Yep, I would have ghosted that hoe, but who am I to say anything when I did my own fucked up shit in life? So, if my dawg loved her dirty panties, I would support his stupid shit no matter what.

"Well, I feel ya, but I was trying to hit you up on some shit. So, a nigga leaving from Vinny's house, and I was talking to Lolita. You know now they saying they caught up with Nadia and they gon handle her for me." I advised him of a portion of the conversation I had with Lolita.

"Nigga, what? The hell you mean they will handle her? The bitch is off her rocker. We need to make sure that situation is dead," Mack sounded more aggravated than I was listening to the shit.

"Exactly, I told Lolita, if the bitch comes near my family, I was putting a bullet in her. What's weird is she acted as if she didn't care about the crazy bitch, and just wanted to get shit back rolling with all the dope, pills and weed. Like I don't think she gives two fucks," I spoke, while I continued to drive in and out of traffic to make it home to Kia. I had been staying home with her to make sure she was ok and safe.

"Nigga, listen no love lost. At least you warned them, so when shit go left, we know how to handle the situation." Mack stated.

"Exactly, what I was thinking nigga, but anyways we have to meet with that nigga Troy to give him and his people they cut and I'm not going to lie those niggas moved that shit quick as hell. You sure you don't want to do business with them niggas?" I asked Mack. I was hoping the nigga said yeah, but I already knew his ego wouldn't let him.

"Nigga, would you do business with Yams if he was alive?" Mack snapped.

"Aiight, nigga I get it damn. I will go meet with them to give them they bread and cut ties. Just know you better be ready to work, because a nigga can't move around like that while I'm still dealing with Kia and the baby." I truthfully told him. Kia barely wanted me to leave her sight.

"Aiight, fam I get it and it's cool. I will keep shit moving for us," He answered. I could tell he was still bothered, by the tone of his voice. I wanted to ask him was he good, but I just wasn't in the mindset to deal with his drama let alone my own.

"Alright, yo. Let me holla at Ricardo and I will meet with you later," I told him.

"Aiight fam," He stated, and we disconnected the call. I dialed Ricardo.

"Yo!" Ricardo answered the phone. "Damn, baby why your shit so loud" I heard a female say in the background.

"Nigga, I hit you at the wrong time," I chuckled.

"Naw, just Amayah" he said as if it wasn't nothing. Amayah was this broad that my brother would kick shit from time to time. She used to be around a lot, until he fell off in Heaven's vagina. Now, I was curious as to what made him start kicking shit with her again.

"Oh, you kicking shit with her these days?"

"I mean, shit, I ain't got no bitch, so I can do as I please bro," he coolly stated. I laughed at my brothers thought process, because he just didn't know what he was getting himself into dealing with Heaven's ass. One thing for sure that I have learned over the years, them damn cousins did not play about the niggas they deal with, and if they wanted you or was into you, you will definitely know. To me, Heaven was the craziest one out of all three of them.

"Well, I want us to meet with Chase so we can link up with Troy and shoot these niggas they bread for handling up and keeping the money product moving." I told him.

"Damn, we can't keep they ass around because shit, they work good as hell and plus a nigga didn't have to do much," he said, and honestly, I agreed with him.

"Yea, I wish, but with Mack and that nigga fucking the same bitch. Ain't shit good coming from that situation." I honestly advised him.

"Shit, these niggas need to worry about the fucking money and fuck these hoes," My brother spoke. He would always freely speak his mind. He didn't care what he said and how it could make someone feel.

"Nigga, easy for you to say until Heaven goes back to Caleb," I jokingly laughed.

"Man, I caught her stupid ass messaging the nigga. I did my part and making sure she was good, but now she about to be put out my shit." I was in complete shocked after my brother spoke on what now made sense as to why he was laid up with Amayah. Heaven must be the dumbest bitch I ever met.

"Nigga, I know yo ass ain't serious. Well shit lets knock the nigga down for what he did," I said ready for whatever.

"Nah, she wanted a nine to five nigga that will beat her ass, so she can keep the nine to five nigga that will beat her ass," My brother said as if he didn't give two fucks about Heaven, but I knew the real him. His feelings were hurt, and a clear indication was the fact he was laid up with Amayah.

"Did you say anything to her about it, Ric?" I asked him. I mean I already knew the answer to this question, but I needed to hear it for myself.

"No, but why do I need to speak on some shit like that? The nigga fucked you up. You were bruised the fuck up and I had to look after you. You can't leave the house and shit because you look fucking crazy. Can't go do shit but, sit up and look at me with your face ugly and shit, because the nigga didn't give a fuck. Then you have the audacity to still be talking to the nigga. Man, that bitch crazy. Ain't that much love in the world could make me that dumb. Right plan wrong nigga. She can pull that dumb shit on him not me," Ric vented. I could tell my brother was really feeling Heaven, but her actions were making him second guess everything. I already knew what was going on because I overheard Kia giving Heaven the business about still communicating with the nigga after Amber's ass snitched on her. I honestly felt bad for my brother because I knew he genuinely cared about Heaven, but if you can't make a person see what is in front of you there is no need trying to force the shit.

"I think you need to talk to her dawg. Let her know where the fuck you coming from, because there is no way a broad I'm fucking going to be in my shit caking with the nigga that got her looking busted and shit. That shit there ain't it." I expressed.

"You right, but I haven't touched Heaven since the night she got fucked up. A niggas not going to be buggin the girl about pussy when she fucked up. Plus, when I saw that shit, I was turned the fuck off. Honestly, I haven't been home since I saw the shit. She keeps calling a nigga, but I don't respond unless she says she need something," he confidently said.

"Wait, so she at your shit why you laid up with the next bitch?" I laughed at how wild my brother could be, but shit this was us. We didn't fall victim to bullshit easily.

"Nigga, I ain't doing shit wrong. She not my girl." He simply said.

"Nigga ain't you laid up with a bitch? Where she at? You just freely talking like this," I curiously asked. The fact he was talking about another woman while laid up with Amayah was some crazy shit to me in a way.

"Man, Amayah don't give a fuck long as I'm here with her," He spoke, and I began to laugh. I could hear a smack in his background.

"Damn, Ric that shit hurt. You always want to play," I could hear Amayah whine in the background.

"Man, listen, you get back to doing you dawg, and I can discuss what I really called you for later," I chuckled at my brother's antics.

"Aiight you, Dum luv," he responded.

"Dum luv," I stated before disconnecting the call. I shook my head at the thought and was happy for once my drama was calming down just a little so, I thought.

GOING IN CIRCLES

Heaven

I got out the steamy hot shower and dried
my body from the dripping water. Once I was done,
I opened the bathroom door to let the steam out, so I
can look in the mirror. While I waited for the mirror
to defog, I rubbed my body with some Rose
pomegranate body butter. I then began to brush my
teeth, floss and rinse my mouth out with Listerine. I
finally looked in the mirror and my bruises were
finally gone from my face. My body still reflected
some small bruising. I sighed deeply because even
though I looked refreshed, I felt depressed. I was
out of a damn job, I was staying in Ricardo's house
and wasn't allowed to go back home, and Caleb
refuses to give me space. I was confused and lost
for the first time in along damn time.

I had finally taken my weave out, so my
long soft relaxed tresses weighed down my back. I
pulled my hair into a high messy bun and sprayed

my face with some rose water and then followed up with a moisturizer. I put on some long sweatpants and a plain white tank. I walked out the bathroom and into the adjourning room. I grabbed my socks and went back into the bathroom to grab the Vaseline. I then went and sat on the bed and rubbed my feet. Putting my socks on. I heard the alarm sound off with the opening of the front door. I already knew who it was, so I quickly straightened up the bathroom and put everything back to how it was and walked out of the room.

"Amber, about time…" I said heading towards the kitchen, but my words got caught in my throat seeing him. He turned around and eyed me down, before turning around and going back to what he was doing. I had not seen Ricardo. It had been two months since the incident and out of nowhere a month ago, he disappeared. He never came back home and would only respond to me by sending me Zelle's or sending screenshots of my bill payments. The nigga took care of me, but I couldn't even return the gesture. I didn't know what set him off to be mad or make him not want to be around me. Far as I knew I didn't do a damn thing. I was waiting on Amber to come back with some groceries so I could cook. I noticed he was counting money. I got so nervous being around him my hands began to sweat. Trying to ease some of my nervousness, I walked around him towards the fridge and grabbed a bottle of water. I then exited the kitchen. I felt like I was holding my breath because of the way I started breathing heavily when I walked out of the kitchen. I went back into the bedroom and got into the bed. I sat my water down on the coaster and turned on the TV. I needed to get my anxiety to subside.

I turned on Hulu and decided to watch *Blackish*. I needed a laugh because right now I was feeling so down. Ricardo finally coming brought my spirits down. The nigga didn't even acknowledge me and I damn sure wasn't going to acknowledge his ass either. I got comfortable under the white and pink comforter. It's crazy how I damn near re-decorated this nigga whole entire house since I've been here. He had new utensils, small kitchen appliances, dishware, glassware and all. I changed out his bedroom comforters and added décor in the bedrooms. I also did the bathrooms over. I knew once he started walking through the house noticing the changes, he was going to be pissed, but I didn't care. He left me alone for a damn month and still was not speaking to me. I sat in the bed in deep thought as the *Blackish* show watched me, because I definitely was not watching the damn TV. I heard his footsteps come closer to the room. When he opened the door, he walked inside and looked around before his eyes landed on me. He then headed for the closet, which I organized as well and added my clothes in there. I just knew this nigga was going to flip about me just taken over his space. Instead, he stripped down to his boxer briefs and walked into the bathroom. I heard the shower come on, and quickly grabbed my cell phone and blocked Caleb so he would not call while Ricardo was home. I then dialed Kia.

"Hello," her voice sounded as if she was awakened from a deep sleep. Just raspy and low.

"Kia, he came home," I whispered in the phone.

"Ok, well did he say anything to you?" She tried to perk up, as she began to yawn.

"No, the nigga didn't say shit, and where the fuck is Amber?" I asked because I had been waiting on her.

"Girl she here next to me sleep. She came to check on me and fell out. I think she tired. She had been running back and forth all day," she advised me.

"Well, she could have told me that. Now my ass is going to starve because she was supposed to bring the groceries," I instantly became annoyed.

"Girl, I don't know what you and Amber arrangement was, but she here sleep. I can wake her up, but you know she going to be cranky as hell. Even Renzo didn't want to wake her ass up. He in the living room laying down. Plus, it is almost 9:30

at night girl, just DoorDash something to eat at this point." Kia informed between her yawns.

"Girl, I don't want shit on there. Ugh, I will eat some cereal. I can't believe she had me waiting like that," I was visibly upset, but I did have to admit; Amber was running her business and running back and forth between Me and Kia.

"So, are you going to speak to him to see why he was acting crazy?" Kia's question took me out my thoughts.

"Um, I don't know if I should. Like nigga if you mad about something then say that shit." I got aggravated even more as I thought about his grown ass being childish.

"Well, bitch if it was me and I was unsure, I would act like shit is normal. Shit nigga you don't say nothing then I won't. Shit, I honestly wouldn't sweat it. The nigga got you laid up in his house and paying the bills at your shit. Girl these non-nine to five niggas can be a headache. Good luck. Better use all that college degree smarts to figure this one out because Renzo ain't telling shit..." Kia stated after being cut off by Amber in the background stating, "And Mack didn't either." We all instantly laughed because we just knew Amber's ass was sleeping.

"Girl the fuck, you eavesdropping," Kia laughed some more.

"Oh, shit the shower cut off. I'm going to call y'all back," I whispered into the phone. I could hear them laughing in the background as I quickly hit the end button and put the phone back on the nightstand. It felt so good to have Kia back home and hearing her laugh. For a long time, she was super paranoid and afraid of every damn thing. I knew she should be delivering the baby any minute now and I couldn't wait. After about five minutes, Ricardo walked out the bathroom with the towel wrapped around him. He went to the drawer and took out some boxer briefs and went into the closet to put the towel in the hamper and put on his boxer briefs. He put a V-neck t-shirt over his head and grabbed things out of his pants pocket, before coming out of the closet. He then sat his phones and his gun on the nightstand. He pulled the blanket back and got in the bed with me, for the first time in a month. He laid flat on his back with his hands behind his head as he glanced at the TV. He sighed deeply like he was finally able to lay and relax. At that moment I was confused as hell. Who the fuck gets missing for a month shows back up home and still don't say shit to the person he left in his damn home?

My frustration was building up and plus my stomach was growling. With that being the excuse, I got up from the bed and headed to the kitchen. I fixed me a bowl of Special K Fruits and yogurt cereal with some coconut milk and sat in the kitchen eating it. I was trying to figure out how I was going to approach this situation. I didn't care what Kia was talking about. Who the fuck can act fucking normal about some shit like that. I finished my cereal in about ten minutes and washed my dishes and then put them in the dishwasher. I had a bad habit of that. I felt like the dishwasher was not going to get everything, so a pre cleaning was a must. I walked back to the bedroom and went into the adjoining bathroom to brush my teeth, floss and rinse my mouth with Listerine again. I changed out of my cotton sweats and tank and put on my big pajama t-shirt that hung on the back of the bathroom door, replacing it with the clothes I had just had on. I then went and got into the bed. I noticed that Ricardo was lightly snoring. I knew then I probably won't get to talk to him at all. I got comfortable in the bed turning on my side making sure my back faced him. I was laying there like that for about fifteen minutes when I felt him scoot closer to the middle of the bed and reached out and pulled me closer to him by my waist. For some reason, I became nervous, and it was like he knew I wanted to say something, because he immediately stopped me.

"Shhh, don't say nothing. I'm tired and I just want to hold you," he whispered in my ear. I could hear him inhale deep into the nape of my neck giving me goosebumps and making my girl downstairs purr and get wet. I decided to listen to him and not say anything, but I knew first thing in the morning I was going to run my mouth. I allowed him to snore in my ear lightly while I watched *Blackish*.

I didn't know how late in the night it was, but his phones started going off. It was one after the other. I was becoming so aggravated I nudged him one good time.

"Hmm what?" he sounded aggravated, but ain't no way he didn't hear the two loud phones going off simultaneously.

"Your phones won't stop ringing," I said to him. He leaned over and I did the same to see who the hell was calling like that. Seeing the name Amayah pop up on his phone made me want to go crazy, but I kept my cool.

"Yo," He answered. I could hear the female speaking but I couldn't make out what she was saying. "Yea, I'm in for the night, but I will catch up with you tomorrow," He yawned and spoke. I heard the female say something else, but I couldn't hear exactly what she was saying. "Aiight," he lastly stated before disconnecting the call. He turned over and was met with me staring at him. "Man don't even say shit to me. A nigga tired as fuck," he got back comfortable and laid back down the same way he was before, but I sat fully up.

"The fuck was that? Like do I need to go back home?" I curiously asked.

"Man don't bother me Heaven. I ain't in the mood," he tried to pull the covers up, but I snatched them back down.

"Then when will you be in the mood, because I haven't seen you," I began to start my shit. I been waiting for this damn moment, I needed answers.

"Heaven, on some real shit, I ain't in the mood because I got pressure with you, so chill that shit out and lay the fuck down before I snap for real." His tone was cold, and it damn sure shut me the fuck up. I laid down frustrated and mad. I scooted closer to the end of the bed to get away from him, but he wasn't having that shit. He pulled me back closer to him and wrapped his legs around me. I tried so hard to doze off, but my mind was going. Like I never had a nigga to shut me up the way Ricardo did, and it was driving me insane. I am usually vocal, but this time I was a mute.

As my thoughts consumed me, I felt Ricardo's hand rub on my butt and thighs. His hand then made it to my wetness. For some reason, my body reacted to Ricardo even when I didn't want it to. It went against me every time. The nigga gently played with my love bud and dipped it inside of me coating his finger with my juices. He went back up playing with my love bud again. I let light moans escape my lips as his tongue tickled my neck followed by his lips doing light suctions. I was feeling my body heat up with pure gratification. He finally leaned over me and made his lips caress mine. He pulled my bottom lip into his mouth sucking on it and then planted kisses all the way down to my breast. Ricardo took his time sucking on every space his lips met on my skin working his way down my breast stomach, until he made it to my opening. He gently let his thick tongue roll around my pearl making me squirm. I let out a sensual moan.

"Damn, you missed daddy huh?" He spoke to my vagina as she became even wetter like she was responding. He began to lap up my juices like it was the last supper. The slurps and sounds that he was making me was turning me on more. The feeling was so electrifying that I began to arch my back deep letting my head go back as further as it could go, and my legs spread wider and wider for him. My right leg began to shake as he continued to devour my precious fruit between my legs. I was feeling the urge of my orgasm when he stopped and shoved his hardness in me making my walls clench and my orgasm explode. My mouth fell agape, from the intensity.

"Breathe baby," he whispered in my ear, making me quiver. Damn, this nigga had a soul snatching dick. I didn't even realize I stopped breathing. I swear I just had an outer body experience. He slowly deep stroked my kitty and it purred with gratitude. I was flowing like a river as he continuously stroked me. Putting my legs over his shoulders he went in deep, and I swear the nigga was winding inside of me like he was on the dance floor in a Jamaican club.

"Aaaahhhh shit!" I let out a scream of pleasure.

"Damn, that's how you feel," his deep baritone voice sent chills down my spine making my juices flow more. "Damn, this shit feels good. You see this shit," he said to me opening my legs wide and making me look down as I watched him slowly going in and out of me while my juices coated his manhood. I swear that shit look so good, that I felt another orgasm building up in me just watching how sexy that shit was looking.

"Hmmmm," I moaned loudly. He began picking up the pace making me contract around his rod more and more.

"Shit, girl stop doing that shit," he clenched his jaw. "Turn around!" he demanded pulling out of me and giving me room to get on all fours. Sliding back in from the back, I gasped at how he filled me up again. Slowly worked my body over as he slapped me on the ass. He leaned into me, making me arch my back deeper as his right hand found my pearl. He slid in and out of me rubbing on my clit. The feeling that was erupting from me had me running like a faucet. I just knew I couldn't take anymore until he had me riding him. I was sliding up and down his pole like a damn pro. When his thumb found my butt, I laid on his chest as he took control, forcing me up and down his pole. I really lost control of all my damn body. With the orgasm that was ripping through me, I couldn't even speak to tell him I was cumming. I felt his dick pulsate and I just knew he coated my walls with his white liquid. We panted as our breathing was erratic. We were stuck, and I was in love. At this point I think if the nigga would have said to jump, I would say how high and how far I should go.

"Dead that shit with Caleb ma. I know you been talking to him. Dead that shit or I'm going to dead him," he spoke as he moved from underneath me and got out the bed, heading towards the shower. Now, it made sense as to why he was mad. The nigga knew I was talking to Caleb. I wanted to object or say something, but this was one of those situations where your nigga was right, and you didn't fight or argue about a situation that really is your fault. I rubbed my hands through my hair and sighed deeply gathering my thoughts. I heard the shower turn on and then he opened the door.

"Get in," he simply stated, and I got my ass up, not wanting to argue with him. I walked inside the bathroom that began to steam up and quickly jumped inside with him. He washed every inch of my body, and I did the same. We dried off and got back in the bed naked. It was still late night, and he gently played in my wet hair as I laid on his chest.

"I mean it Heaven. Dead that shit. No ties to that nigga, because honestly I'm sparing him because your silly ass still got love for him, but dead that shit. You mine now and he can't have you." He firmly spoke. I nodded my head in understanding. It seemed like I didn't have a say so, and I wasn't going to rebuttal because I had finally got my best friend back and if he didn't want me to speak with Caleb's crazy ass then so be it. The problem was deeper than that though and only time will tell how this shit was really going to play out, because something told me I was going to be in some deep shit with Caleb.

FINALLY, IT'S TIME

Kia

I was on bedrest since the incident and was
not allowed to go to the damn grocery store. Renzo
was so scared I was going to have this baby that he
would fly off the handle if I did too much work
around the house. I wasn't allowed to clean or cook
half the damn time. When I left the hospital, Renzo
made sure to move me into another home. I'm not
sure how he pulled it off, but by the time I got out
the hospital, Amber had me moved way out west
and the place was fully decorated with the nursery
fully decorated as well. I was in love with my new
home, and I appreciated my cousin knowing my
style and decorating each room with a look she
knew I would approve. I sat lounging on the couch
in the den trying to decide what to watch on the 80-
inch flatscreen TV, as I scrolled through Hulu. I
was finally in my last month and I was big as a
house. I felt like I would burst at any given moment.

I honestly was happy that I made this far keeping the seed of chuckie inside. I heard Amber in the kitchen trying to cook a meal while arguing with Mack. This was a never-ending cycle with these two. I heard the front door open and the alarm going off. I could hear the alarm code being put in. I sat there patiently waiting for Renzo's face to appear in the living room. He walked in and I could see the worry in his face, which alarmed me. When he realized I was staring at him he smirked at me.

"Damn, you were waiting on a nigga," He cockily responded. I rolled my eyes and laughed at the thought.

"Man, bye I was not waiting on you, but I'm just happy to see you," I said for the first time in a long time. My paranoia had calmed down just a little and I was no longer feeling as scared. I still always needed someone in the house with me and my gun close. This shit I went through made me so cautious of people. I questioned everything and every person.

"Damn, I didn't hear that from you in a long time," he dropped his keys on the table and sat next to me on the couch lifting my feet up as he began to rub them. Damn that shit felt good. They had become a little swollen and the pressure his hands applied made me feel so comfortable and good.

"Yea, I guess I miss you," I smiled. Amber came walking in with the plate of food she cooked. I had to admit, it was looking really good. My mouth began watered. I was able to keep foods down now, and my body was officially handling the pregnancy well. Amber handed me my plate and I looked at the roasted herb chicken thighs, lemon garlic butter broccoli and homemade herb mash potatoes smelled delectable. My mouth watered and my baby did backflips.

"You want a plate Renzo?" Amber asked him.

"Yea, damn Amber you might have to move in permanently." Renzo got excited about his food.

"I bet. Do you want me to put up all the gifts and stuff for the baby and get your hospital bag ready?" Amber asked. I wanted to do it myself, but I knew it was just too much for me to do. I thought it was sweet that Amber arranged for a drive by gift drop off since we didn't get to do the gender reveal or the baby shower. She had a decorated station where people received small thank you favors and finger foods as they drove by and dropped off the gifts for my unborn. I had got so many things, I don't think we needed anything else. Shit we had damn near four of everything. Amber's silly ass didn't want to take nothing back, talking about the baby will have everything he or she needs at everyone's house. I just shook my head. I think they were more excited about the baby then me.

"Yea, it's fine. I'm going to sit here and relax anyways," I said to her.

"Cool," she said walking away back to the kitchen. After about five minutes she was walking back with Renzo's plate of food. She then went back in the kitchen and came back with two coasters and sat the drinks down. This was our routine every evening. Amber would cook and she would fix our plates and give Renzo and I our space and alone time. Renzo and I began digging into our food. I don't think either one of us wanted to stop and have casual talking in between bites. Once we were done, he grabbed my plate and went into the kitchen. I could hear the water running in the kitchen and could tell he was washing the dishes. After about ten minutes, he was walking back and sitting on the couch again, propping my feet up. I heard the doorbell ring and looked at him with curiosity of who that might be. Renzo shrugged his shoulders and got up to see who it was. I heard him open the door.

"Where she at?" the sounds of Mack's voice put me at ease. He came walking in, but I knew he was mad about something. His face wore a scowl, and he just nodded his head at me. He normally would speak but tonight he just nodded his head. He headed to the room Amber was in and the yelling erupted. Renzo sat down next to me and all we could do was shake our head these two continuously got into it and the fussing and fighting had become an everyday thing between the two. Amber was hurt and being vindictive, while Mack tried to put up with his nagging ass baby mama and Amber's crazy ass actions.

"You think they would take this shit to their house," I was clearly annoyed and tired of hearing the arguing.

"Man, your cousin has done some crazy shit again," Renzo shook his head. I didn't even want to know what she had done now, because the girl was half crazy if you asked me.

"So, changing all my fucking account info and moving my fucking bread so I don't have no money, ain't being spiteful!" I heard Mack yell. I looked at Renzo in shock and he shook his head like *yeah bitch I told you*. I swear he look like he did that shit just like a female all he was missing was the snaps of the fingers. I fell out laughing as he chuckled too.

"You think that bitch about to mooch off you? You must be out of your damn mind! You gave the bitch a fucking card! To spend what? Not the money we worked for! Nigga give her the drug money you got stashed in the house in Weston!" Amber screamed and Renzo looked at me in shock.

"Oh, her ass found his stash spot," I said to Renzo, and he looked at me like *how the fuck this girl found that?*

"Bitch, you been following me!" we heard Mack yell. At that point, our nosey asses cut the TV volume down, to make sure we caught all the tea and shade from their Lipton tea palm tree asses.

"Nigga, I goes where the money resides and if that means making sure that hoe don't get not one red cent from something I helped build then so be it! Got me fucked up. You want to put babies in ex's and shit but give me hell when I want to be friends with a nigga…"

"Man, I should beat your stupid ass! Amber my money better be back in my account tomorrow, or…" Mack bellowed.

"Or fucking what? Nigga kiss my ass where it don't shine and make sure you lick my booty hole! I take care of everything and since your stupid ass don't know not to give your baby mama your fucking card, I will be delegating shit from now on! I'm going to be handling all the affairs, that bitch work she can take care of herself. all we need to do is take care of Maliyah and if she can't do that shit right, I will gladly take Maliyah permanently! Y'all got the wrong bitch with the wrong plan! Play with my pussy not my intelligence!" Amber yelled before slamming the room door. You could hear her stomping into the bathroom.

"We're so damn nosey." I said to Renzo.

"Honestly, them niggas in your house loud as fuck," he shrugged, and I began to laugh hysterically. He was right though we didn't have to do much to hear them two going at it.

"You want me to run your bath?" Renzo asked, and I nodded my head yes. Renzo got up to go run my bath water. He had become so attentive to me and my needs. It's funny how we never discussed getting back together or talked about a relationship. We kind of just lived within the moment and that was fine with me. I wasn't thinking about a relationship at this moment. I just was ready to meet my baby, and then figure out my life after. Mack walked out of Amber's room, and I could see the stress wearing on him. These two women of his was driving him crazy. I watched him go to my mini bar that held all Renzo's favorite liquor because it definitely wasn't my liquor that Renzo went and stocked up on. He grabbed the D'usse bottle and pour it into the glass and then took the drink straight to the head.

"Mack she is hurt, and she is trying to deal and process that not only do you have a daughter, but you have another child on the way. She is hurt and it's the fact she thought that you both were going to be each other first when it came to being parents. I think has her a little on edge. Word of advice instead of fighting with Amber give her reassurance and show her how much you love her and you are dedicated to making it work. On some real shit if she still can't respect you having to be a good father whether it is to help your BM, then you need to re-evaluate what is important. Not saying you right, but y'all need to determine boundaries if y'all are going to be together," I offered my advice. I got up to head to my bedroom leaving Mack to his thoughts. Since Amber been with me out of the hospital, she and Mack have been going at it and my cousin has been on a vindictive tirade. She wanted to make Mack pay and I honestly felt like for what. They both were to blame in for their actions and roles they played in their drama.

Walking into my bedroom. I began to undress. Once I was fully naked, I stared at my smooth round stomach. I had light stretchmarks on the sides of my stomach, but there were only a few of them on each side of my stomach. I smiled at the fact I could see the small movements in my stomach from the baby moving around. It felt weird carrying a whole little human inside of you, but the love I had I knew I couldn't wait to share the same air with this baby. I stood there for a moment and when Renzo open the door he stood there for a few moments in awe.

"Damn, this shit so raw. The fact you still look damn good with a whole baby inside of you is amazing as hell." He gawked.

"You want to feel the baby move?" I asked him. He nodded his head yes and walked over to me. He stood in front of me and placed his hand on my stomach. The baby began to kick everywhere Renzo moved his hand.

"Damn, lil nigga knows it's his daddy," Renzo chuckled in Amazement.

"How do you know it's a he?" I asked laughing.

"Because he gave you hell, just like his daddy," he stated with all seriousness, and I began to hysterically laugh at his humor.

"Nigga, you foolish for real." I continued laughing.

"You ready to get in the tub?" he asked and helped me in the tub. The huge dual whirlpool tub had my body feeling so good, as I leaned my head back.

I felt Renzo's strong hands began to massage my shoulders and arms. He then sat on the edge of the tub and began to bathe me. When I say the nigga was a whole different person since I came out the hospital it was crazy. He was so attentive and careful. He made sure he was here no later than 9:30pm, making sure everything was good with me. I sometimes would tell him he could go home, but I would just find him sleep on my living room sofa with his gun next to him. I think the situation made him just as cautious and paranoid as me. Especially since they have not found the bitch yet. Once I was out the tub and dried, Renzo rubbed me down with my body butter. He massaged me down, making sure my body didn't feel over worked and strained. He decided to watch a movie with me and before I dozed off and he left out the room. My paranoia still got the best of me because I made sure to put my gun under the other pillow next to me before I fell into a deep sleep. He could say what he wanted, but I had this gut feeling that bitch was not done and was coming back for me.

Waking up, I leaned over to grab my phone. I hit the button on the side to see the time. Seeing it was 11 o'clock, I sat the phone down and rub my eyes. I could feel my baby moving making me smile. I slowly got up and stretched. I got up and walked out of the room and headed towards the kitchen. I saw Renzo laid out on the couch sleeping. He was slightly snoring, and his phone was going off. For some reason I wanted to go pick it up to see who it was, because since we have been around each other the phone barely rings unless it is Mack, Ricardo, Chase, Amber or Heaven. It was too early for anyone to be calling him at this time. I was just about to be nosey and go look when loudmouth ass Amber came out of the bedroom.

"No! I told you that if he was late one more time he was fired! Mack, stop giving people chances when they are costing money." She yelled into the phone.

"Girl, ssshhh!" I shushed her in hopes of her lowering the volume on her vocals. Renzo's eyes popped open. He stretched and yawn, closing his eyes back again.

"Shut the fuck up Amber damn! You and that nigga been fussing all night and now it's morning and you still fucking fussing!" Renzo snapped. I giggled because one thing for sure the nigga hated being awaken out his sleep.

"Man, fuck you," Amber yelled at Renzo.

"That's probably what your ass needs to be doing. Withholding pussy from Mack is only going to make the nigga go fuck Tina's ass," Renzo antagonized Amber while he continued to lay on the couch with his eyes closed. Amber walked over to the couch and punched Renzo in his chest making him scrunch in pain, coughing. I began to laugh so hard at that point those two would always fight or go at it. I began holding my stomach as I continued to laugh. I then felt a sharp pain followed by water trickling down my leg. I knew damn well I didn't pee. As Amber and Renzo continued to fuss back and forth, I began to try and see what the hell I had going on and what just happened. I went to walk to the bathroom and pressure I felt made me stop and hold my stomach. I began to breathe through it. I didn't feel any pain but just a lot of pressure.

"Umm, guys!" I yelled making them both look at me.

"Girl did you just piss on the floor?" Amber's ditsy ass said.

"No, dumb ass girl. She done went into labor," Renzo jumped up grabbing my arm gently.

"Oh shit! Oh shit!" Amber began to panic.

"Amber, why your silly ass panicking? The girl ain't even yelling," Renzo looked at her as if she was crazy.

"Man, fuck you nigga. Go get her ready and I'm going to grab the hospital bag." Amber moved quickly to go grab my hospital bag.

"C'mon let's get you cleaned up," Renzo made sure to let me put majority of my weight on him as he helped me walk down the hall. Once we made it into the bedroom, Renzo helped me take a bath and put on my clothes. I never felt pain, just a whole lot of pressure going down. Once I was completely ready, we all got in Renzo's new 2019 Lincoln Nautilus Black Label. The truck was really nice, and I had to admit I was shocked he settled for a Lincoln, because being with Nadia, the nigga turned bourgeois really quick on us. As we drove to the hospital, I felt a sharp pain in my stomach. It almost felt like I was cramping. I winced in pain and started to breathe through it.

"You good Kia?" Amber asked me.

"Um, I'm ok I just felt a sharp pain, but it subsided," I told her.

"Don't you need to time them?" Renzo looked over at me and reached over to rub my stomach.

"Yes, you right if I have another one… shit!" I yelped. I was more so caught off guard.

"Ok, breathe and start timing them," Amber said, like she was a coaching midwife.

"I know that Amber," I became instantly aggravated with her.

"I'm just trying to help damn," Amber sneered and sat back in her seat.

"Y'all can fuss later. Kia we getting close, so just continue to do what you doing shawty," Renzo continued to rub my stomach, while using his other hand to steer the wheel.

We made it to the hospital and Renzo quickly got me inside and had the truck valeted. They rushed me to the third floor and soon as I stepped foot in triage. The nurses began to surround me.

"Hello Kia, I'm your nurse Sonja. I am going to check you to see how far dilated you are." The nurse told me and nodded my head yes. She put the gloves on and lubricated her hand. She then slowly stuck her finger inside me and placed her hand on my stomach. She then looked surprised.

"Are you in any pain?" she asked.

"No just a lot of pressure," I simply said.

"Hmm, that's weird your already about 6 ½ cm. Let me get you hooked up and monitored with an IV bag to see what your contractions are looking like," she simply said and got up quickly. I watched her dictate orders to the other nurses. They got me into my room quickly at that point and started hooking the monitors up around my belly, chest and arms. They continued to monitor my blood pressure closely because of my past issues during my pregnancy. A nurse was checking in on my every ten minutes. Renzo got comfortable and was in the bed with me rubbing my stomach to make sure I was comfortable.

According to the nurse I was dilating fast, and my blood pressure was normal, but my contractions was coming up in the system off the charts. The nurse said I should be screaming. I felt the pains, but they only felt like a stomachache and that I needed to take a long bathroom break that included me getting in the shower after. I heard the door open and in walked in Amber, Heaven, Mack, Ricardo, and Chase.

"Well look at y'all two big asses just lying in one small ass bed together," Chase voice made me look up. I swore it was the nurse coming in.

"Nigga, they let all y'all asses up?" Renzo slid out of the bed with me.

"You know Memorial is geared to family birthing. That's why the room is the size of a damn hotel," Amber said walking to the pull-out couch that Renzo was supposed to lay in.

"Well, when she gets ready to push all y'all niggas getting out. Y'all not about to watch Kia's pussy on full display," Renzo's seriously told them, and the guys was amused.

"Nigga it's Kia's pussy now that it's being stretched like the size of a watermelon," Chase laughed.

"It be you dawg that got to be so ignorant," Amber rolled her eyes while Chase laughed.

"How are you feeling?" Heaven walked up to me, rubbing my arm.

"I mean it don't hurt like I imagined it would. I don't think I will need any pain meds though, just a lot of pressure," I honestly told her. I noticed the bruising was gone and she looked brand new, but something was bothering her. I know my cousin. She becomes very reserved when something is bothering her.

"Well, I hope you have an easy delivery," she smiled. Yep, something was clearly wrong. She was not making jokes like she would normally do, just damn reserved. I wanted to call her out on it, but the pressure I was feeling started to intensify.

"Man, y'all niggas mad annoying," Amber snapped walking towards me and Heaven. "You good Heaven?" Amber asked. I knew she picked up on her vibe too.

"Yea, I'm good," she smiled. Yep, again this bitch was lying.

"Hmph, Ric beating you too? You know you can tell us we will beat his ass," Amber's wild ass said trying to whisper it so the guys would not hear her. I couldn't help but to chuckle, but Heaven found it more amusing.

"Girl, hell no. If anything he treats me really good, but I do think I may have a hoe problem," she rolled her eyes and looked back at him, while him and the guys were talking.

"Girl hmphed, don't they all. Shit I think Mack done started back messing with his BM,"

Amber's retarded ass said. Heaven and I instantly rolled our eyes because we knew Mack's ass been following behind her like a sick puppy and the BM been acting an ass because she can barely get the nigga to get his Jit.

"Girl, shut up. The nigga been so far up your ass he ain't even been a good damn daddy," Heaven said what I wanted to say.

"Not my problem he went and had an outside baby" Amber shrugged.

"Shit you a dead beat too. That little girl was calling you mommy too," I said making Heaven scream in laughter while Amber mugged me and stuck the middle finger.

"Bitch I hope that baby fuck yo pussy up, over here talking shit," Amber got salty and walked away from the bed making the boys look over at us.

"Aye, stop wishing shit like that on her," Renzo chimed in.

"Oh, so now you care what's gon happen to the pussy when it's your turn to go back in it," Chase said making everyone laugh, except me.

Ain't shit funny about my pussy being fucked up. A nurse came in, that we didn't know, but I had to admit she was fine as hell. She looked young, but she was so damn pretty. She reminded me of Alexis Skyy just a little slimmer in her structure, but she was still curvaceous. She had deep dimples because even when she spoke, they appeared in her face instantly.

"Hello everyone, I'm Karina. I will be the one checking your vitals while you're here. I will add my name and pager number as well if you ever need any help. I will also put the charge nurse name and information as well," she smiled warmly and went to the dry erase board to put her information on their.

"Damn, can you check my vitals please? I don't think I'm breathing," Chase began to bother her, and we all laughed because she just didn't know what she was about to be aggravated with.

"Um, sure when you pass out," she chuckled, but when Chase's ass fell on the floor like he passed out for real, we all cried laughing. This nigga was stupid. Karina was in shock and her dumb ass really kneeled to the floor to make sure the nigga was ok, but when he opened his eyes with his head in her lap he smiled, and she couldn't do anything but laugh. After harassing her for ten minutes we learned she was twenty and was in school for nursing while working as an LPN. It was amazing because she was so young, but after she broke down how she did dual enrollment and went to technical school after graduating, it was easy for her to become an LPN with already having majority of her credits early. She took my vitals and after sitting with us for a few more minutes she left with Chase following right behind her.

"We going to leave before you got to start cocking your big ass legs up," Ricardo said making me roll my eyes.

"Yes, please because a nigga like me ain't got the stomach for that shit," Mack stated.

"Do you want us to go?" Amber asked.

"Honestly, I just wanted it to be us, but I will call y'all soon as the baby is born," I expressed, and she nodded her head in understanding. Heaven gave me a hug and they all walked out the door.

"How are you feeling?" Renzo asked.

"I'm starting to feel a lot more pressure and the pains are starting to increase," I told him.

"Want me to rub you or get you something?" He was so genuine lately and attentive that I kind of sat there staring at him in amazement. I don't know how I was feeling but this was making me fall for the smooth ass nigga all over again.

"Um, no I just need to lay here," I responded. "The pressure is getting worse," I continued after moaning from the intensity of the pressure I felt pushing down my pelvic area.

"You sure you don't want me to get the nurse?" He asked.

"Noooo, oh shit. It's like my body is making me want to push. It feels so heavy." I tried to explain to him what I was feeling. The empathy that showed on Renzo's face let me know that he was sorry I was going through this.

"Kia, um let me just call the nurse. You probably need to be checked," Renzo said in fear. He walked quickly out the door to get the nurse. I rolled on my back, and I could feel a sharp pain come down towards my vagina. I started to feel the pressure even more as I gripped the side of the bed railing. "Hmmmm shit!" I said low enough for me to hear only. After about what felt like five minutes Renzo came back in with the nurse. My legs were gapped open and the minute the nurse came in I could tell from her facial expression something was definitely wrong or happening.

"Oh shit!" he shouted. Making me become extremely nervous. He rubbed his face in nervousness.

"What's wrong?" I began to panic.

"I'm sorry just breathe Kia, I need you not to push and to stay as calm as possible. If you feel a contraction do not push, just try to breathe through it," she explained.

"The hell you mean don't push? It's my body doing it. I can't stop this big head baby from coming," I yelled amid me having a huge contraction.

"I know and I'm so sorry your labor is moving rather quicker than we thought. Just let me get your doctor in here," she said quickly walking out of the room to get the nurse.

"Yo, I don't know if a nigga could never look at you the same. The way this lil baby got your pussy spread wide is fucking disgusting." Renzo expressed as he stood in front of me watching in horror.

"Oh, nigga you the reason I'm in this predicament! Aaaahhhhhh!" I yelled out in pain for the first time. "Oh shit, why is it hurting now?" I laid my head back and began to take deep breaths. A gang of nurses came in the room, with my doctor and Chase's ass right behind them. He was too excited, as he had his phone out recording the whole ordeal. He came back in because he had to be following the nurse that came in to check my vitals.

"Damn, that baby head is big! The fuck you were eating carrying that lil seed of fucking

Chuckie" Chase's ass cried out making some of the nurses laugh.

"Someone better get Chase before I get up and beat his ASSSSSSS!" I could barely finish as I felt the worst pain in my life push down on my vagina. "Jesus I'm so sorry for all the hell I brought on this earth. I'm so sorry Renzo for being so mean to your little seed of Chuckie. Jesus just please make it stop," I whined like Jesus was there in the flesh.

"Girl don't say sorry now. Your ass should have never let that nigga put his demon nut in you. Now look at yo ass asking Jesus to help you with the demon spawn!" Chase cackled.

"Y'all let me the fuck up!" I roared trying to get out of the bed to get to Chase's ass.

"Kia, calm down you can't move you're going to snap the baby's neck. I just need you to take deep breaths and listen to me and me only," my doctor said. "Renzo can you please go comfort her instead of staring?" My doctor was just as irritated with him and Chase as I was.

"Oh, my fault, but damn why it looks like that?" he paused as the baby's head came out.

"Kia, I'm going to suction his mouth, but I need you to do a big push to get his shoulders out," The doctor said. I could hear them suctioning the baby's mouth. "Alright come on one big push when you have a contraction," she coached me.

"Ugggghhhh," I pushed during my contraction. I could feel Renzo's hand in mine and felt his lips hit my forehead.

"Oh, shit that lil muthafucka got a big dick for a baby," Chase yelled out alerting us it was a boy. The fact the whole room laughed, and I could finally breathe gave me a sense of relief. I looked up at Renzo with a faint smile, but his eyes showed concern.

"Kia, something's wrong!" Renzo yelled, and that was the last words I heard before everything went black.

STARTING OVER

Renzo

I held my son in my arms and couldn't believe that God allowed me to see this even when I thought I wasn't going to. He stared at me with his deep brown eyes. He moved his mouth making his dimples pierce through both sides of his cheeks. Kia gave birth to a healthy 9 pound and 8 ounces baby boy. This was my little nigga, Renzo Amir Wright Jr. Damn the little nigga looked exactly like me, down to the birthmark behind his ear like mine. He only carried Kia's mocha complexion, full shaped lips, and her curly hair that swirled all over his head. I was in pure love. I cradled him as he stirred in my arms. I knew what he wanted, but Kia had not awakened yet. She had passed out from hemorrhaging badly. They wanted to do a hysterectomy, but I just couldn't agree to that. I begged them to try their best to let that be the last option. I could never agree to letting them do something that will take away her right as a woman. They had worked on getting the hemorrhaging under control and stop the excessive bleeding. We just didn't know when she would wake up. For some reason they had took her off the sedation, but she had not woken up yet. I was scared as fuck to go home alone with a newborn. I would have needed both my mama, Kia's mom, and aunties there to help me. I didn't know shit about taking care of no baby and was hoping she would wake up soon.

"Am I allowed to go back in the room with the baby to see if mom is up?" I asked the nurse.

"Sure, let me get you set up first." The nurse smiled at me. I knew that smile from anywhere, but I was not about to feed into the bullshit. I had enough going on. My phone began to vibrate in my pocket. I pulled it out with my left hand as I continued to hold the baby in my right hand. I looked at the caller ID and ignored it. Seeing it was nothing of importance, I put the phone back in my pocket and continued to cradle my son.

"Ok, here you can push him in this, but let me show you how to change him again." The nurse sweetly said. She went over everything again far as holding him, how to feed him and how to change him. Not sure why she felt the need to do all that. A nigga wasn't dumb, but I figured little mama just wanted to be in a niggas face. Some women didn't care who the nigga belong to as long as they could have a piece too.

I finally walked down the hall to Kia's room. She was peacefully sleeping with her eyes closed. She had been like this since yesterday evening. She looked peaceful her once big stomach was now gone. The nurse Chase ended up talking to, came in and wrapped her stomach and made sure she was always good, just to look out. I moved the baby's bed closer to her and picked him up again. I walked around the room and looked at all the gifts that everyone sent her. I noticed there was a new gift with a big red bow on it and a red balloon that said get well soon. I walked over to examine it but hearing Kia's voice made me turn around quickly.

"Renzo," she said. "Renzo." She began to cough and moan like she felt pain. I walked over to her bedside. "Was that you that came in?" she asked looking at me.

"Yea, I just got here what's wrong?" I asked with concern.

"You sure you just came in here, I thought I saw someone in here," she said with her eyes barely open.

"I think it was the medication, Kia. No one was in here when I walked in," I looked around the room and didn't see anything out of the ordinary.

"Um, my throat is dry," she said. Her voice cracked every time she spoke. I nodded my head and walked towards the door and opened it.

"Hey, can one of y'all bring her something to drink? She finally woke up." I shouted enough for them to hear me at the nurse's station. I saw one of the nurses get up quickly and headed in my direction. I went back inside the room and carried the baby near her.

"Can I see him? How long have I been sleep?" she asked, trying to sit up and winced in pain.

"You started hemorrhaging and lost a lot of blood. They almost had to do a blood transfusion and wanted to do a hysterectomy," I advised her. Her eyes got big, and she felt her wrapped stomach.

"What the fuck? I thought I just fell asleep. Wait I can't have more kids?" The sadness showed on her face.

"Not sure, but I didn't let them do the hysterectomy. They just did shit the old fashion way, so your doctor said." I told her what I did know.

"Hello Kia, good to see you are finally awake. We were worried you were not going to wake up. We were just about to add your feeding tube today. Never had a patient take so long to wake up. Let me check your vitals and make sure you're bleeding normally now." The nurse said to her. As she began to work on her, I sat in the chair next to Kia so I could lay the baby on my chest and hold her hand. Once the nurse was done, she began to tell her how to care for herself and that they needed her to start getting up to walk around, and how she needed to at least make one bowel movement. I tell you one thing, I had a new respect for women and the next time I had another baby, I would ask the women first if it was ok, because this shit they go through is on a different level.

"We pumped your breast because we weren't sure if you would want to breast feed and we didn't want you to wake up and still have some of the medication in your system, so we did a pump and dump. You can still try and get him to latch on. I'm just going to have you sit up." She stated helping Kia try and sit up. "You're going to be in some pain because we had to press down a lot on your stomach and scrape out the placenta since it broke up inside of you." She continued. Kia nodded her head in agreement.

"I'm going to help you latch your son on, and then once he is done feeding, I'm going to help you walk around for a bit, ok?" the nurse advised

Kia who nodded her head again. The nurse gently took my son out of my hands and placed it in hers. He squirmed against Kia, and I swear we seen him smile exposing his dimple, making the nurse and Kia say, "Aww!"

"Well, it looks like he was waiting on you," the nurse stated, right before she quickly grabbed Kia's breast and stuffed it in his mouth. The way she did that shit so fast you could tell she do this daily. The way that little nigga started sucking I knew he was a breast boy.

"Is it supposed to hurt like this?" Kia winced in pain.

"Your nipple will be sensitive, and your stomach will contract, but that will help you lose that stomach quicker and dropped the rest of that baby weight," she advised.

"Ok, look Renzo he is smiling and staring at me," she looked at him in awe.

"Ok, I will give you guys some privacy. I will be back to get you guys to move around."

"Damn, he is so handsome, like he looks just like you," Kia gawked at our son. "What's wrong?" she asked looking at me with concern.

"Nothing, a nigga simply happy you ok. I thought I was going to be by myself and I ain't gon lie, shit scared me. Then they weren't sure what was going to happen to you. A nigga was scared." I truthfully told her.

"Well, don't worry yourself I'm here. I guess God knew you would fuck up," she laughed and then winced again in pain.

"I'm going to text your cousins to let them know you good," I told her pulling out my phone from my pocket. I noticed I got a message from someone and decided to get back to the message later. I texted Amber and Heaven.

"What did you name him?" she asked.

"Simple, he a Jr." I smiled big and proud.

"Nigga, you named my child after you?" she frowned.

"The hell that's supposed to mean?" I frowned as well feeling offended.

"Nigga my son going to be already fucked up with your bad genes now he got to have your name? Oh hell naw," she snapped, and I chuckled because she knew damn well, she was happy to have my first baby and name him after me. "Glad you find this shit funny sir." She leaned her head back and closed her eyes slightly as she held our son as he still sucked or her breast.

"You good ma?" I asked her.

"Yea just feel drained all of a sudden," she said and began to yawn, as someone burst through the door.

"Family!" Chase loud ass yelled walking through the door.

"Nigga you don't knock or ask if you can come?" Kia rolled her eyes.

"Girl you my sister now. I done seen you bust it wide open, and I do mean literally. That nigga head was so damn big," He laughed.

"Nigga leave the damn girl alone," I dapped Chase's silly ass up.

"Man, for real. The nurse was like you didn't tear, what the fuck that mean? Y'all women pussies be breaking and shit when y'all push them big head babies out?" Chase seriously asked making Kia laugh hysterically. I looked at her and shit I'm not going to lie I wanted to know too. A nigga did not know shit about giving birth.

"What the fuck. You can't be this dumb," Kia laughed. Chase shrugged his shoulders and walked over towards her and the baby.

"Damn, the nigga starting early sucking on tits and shit." Chase unfiltered mouth continued.

"Nigga shut up!" I laughed at his dumbass.

"No, I'm breastfeeding him. Where is your nurse boo?" Kia was trying to get in his business.

"Man, she around I'm trying to bust her ass if she will let a nigga," he bluntly spoke making me and Kia laugh.

"Nigga, you need to stop and leave that grown woman alone," Kia advised him, making fun of the fact the nurse was older than chase.

"Damn, the little nigga looks just like you Renzo," Chase said admiring my son while Kia breastfed.

"Nigga, thank you, but you too damn close to Kia and her exposed breast," I told his young ass.

"Oh, my fault, but I wouldn't dare. Plus after seeing what came out of her I could never," Chase turned his nose up, making me laugh and Kia suck her teeth with an attitude. The door opened again letting Amber and Heaven walk in. They walked in super excited as they drooled over the baby before them. After about twenty minutes Mack and Ricardo came walking in. We all sat at the hospital for over two hours laughing and talking. Chase left first followed by Ricardo and Heaven.

"Hey, I want to go home and change clothes and get dressed. Can y'all stay here with her?" I asked Mack and Amber. Amber nodded her head in agreement. Kia had finally dozed off and my little man was in Amber's arms sleep. I dapped Mack up and walked out of the room door and down to the valet area. I waited for my car to pull up. My phone rang seeing who it was I answered.

"Hey, how is everything?" she sweetly sang.

"Everything was good. Listen I'm going to hit you up after I grab some clothes from my house and shower." I told the female on the other line.

"Ok, no problem," she sweetly said before we disconnected the call. Getting in the truck I drove to grab me something to eat first from Outback Steakhouse really quick. A nigga was starving. I felt like I have not eaten in days, but it had only been for twenty-four hours since I was too worried about Kia. Getting out the car after parking, I went inside and placed my order. I grabbed me a drink at the bar while I waited. I sat there reflecting on the shit we had been through and finally being free of these demons. The waiter brought out my food and I paid for it. I walked in the parking lot heading to my whip, when a black Escalade drove by so close to me that it almost hit me. Had I not jumped out the way I would have been hit. Staring at the car in the distance I cursed at it. I knew I was not going to make it to my car intime to catch the damn truck. I was too mad, like people never watched where the hell they were going. I got in my truck and drove to my house where all my shit was. I took a hot shower quickly and packed a bag so that I could go be at the hospital with Kia and then go home with her for a few days. I left and made a detour before the hospital. I pulled up to the A.P. T's and sent a text on my phone. After a few minutes, she came walking down with her reading glasses on her face, and her real hair hanging down in a wrap. She looked different and her aura was different. Going through the shit I was going through me and her became real good friends. I unlocked the door as she got in and leaned over giving me a kiss on the cheek.

"What's up? How is Kia? Did she wakeup?" she asked. I probably knew she wasn't being really sincere, but a nigga needed a friend after all the shit I went through with Kia.

"She is ok, thanks for asking," I advise her.

"So really how are you feeling? I know you, you seem lost," She expressed with concern.

"I mean a nigga just trying to grasp the fact I'm a dad and a protector now. You know a nigga got to really figure this shit out. I can't be doing this shit all my life." I began to break down my weed that I pulled from my pocket, that was now was in my lap.

"Look, shit will figure itself out. Right now you need to be enjoying the joys of being a father. Everything will fall into place." She tried her best to give me encouraging words but for some reason the doubt hung over my head heavy these days.

"Thanks for being there for a nigga," I looked up at her. She smiled big.

"You know I got you. I mean we friends right?" Her comment was suggestive.

"A nigga been spending a lot of time with Kia. How you feelin' about all this?" I decided to ask her. I wanted to be as honest as possible with the women in my life from here on out. The only person I did not express shit to was Kia. That was because we had already agreed to co-parent and not be in a relationship while she was pregnant. This was before the incident of her getting kidnapped. Kia had made it clear as to what she wanted from me. Now, sitting in front of this girl, I didn't want her to feel no type of way, but I have been definitely hearing it in her voice the more we spent time together. People may feel like I probably shouldn't be talking to her, but what is a nigga supposed to do be alone while Kia figure out if it's me she wants.

"I mean, what can I feel? I knew what it was when we started talking. Nothing has changed. We are forever going to be friends. You say you and Kia are only co-parenting, I can only trust that is what you are trying to do. I mean I care about you a lot and would love more, but I know now it's just a friend thing until you're sure of what you want." She spoke her truth. I just finished rolling the weed and lit it. I pulled on the blunt deep and held my breath in deep, before releasing the thick cloud of smoke out slowly.

"Well, I told you what it is. I don't sleep in the room with her or nothing because I don't want to confuse shit, but I also don't want to confuse you, so for now we rocking how we rocking." I honestly told her. She nodded her head in agreement and took the blunt from me. We sat in the car passing each other the blunt and talking about any and everything together. It was weird she had become my human diary and most people, let alone a female could not do that, but she did every time. I sat staring out the tinted windows, as we kept smoking. I knew for sure I thought I saw all black figure of someone's silhouette in the distance, but when I sat up and tried to focus on it, the silhouette was gone. Damn, that shit was weird.

BACK AT IT AGAIN

Heaven

It had been over a month since Kia gave birth. We all decided to have dinner at her house, and I had agreed to cook. I needed to pick up somethings from the store. I walked up and down the isles looking for the things that I needed. My phone rang interrupting my train of thought as I tried to figure out what else I needed from the store before I checked out. Seeing it was Ricardo made me smile. Ever since he made me basically choose him, I have been really enjoying my life. He has been the sweetest thug I ever met. The nigga was straight soft for me. If I whined for anything, he was coming to my rescue. He never wanted me to want for nothing. My birthday was days away and I just could imagine what he was getting me. Grabbing my phone, I slide the button on the screen.

"Hey baby," I sweetly answered.

"Heav! You still in the store," he aggravatedly questioned. He nicknamed me Heav because he would say *"I'm tired of saying Heaven all of the time."*

"Yes, what you want? And why you always got an attitude when I leave?" I began to laugh because the nigga almost sounded like he was whining too.

"A nigga hungry and ready to go. I been in this shit starving because all your ass buy is healthy shit," he complained.

"Ricardo, go eat some grapes or an apple. Stop complaining and eat it. It's good for you. Plus, you must meet me at Kia's house anyways. I'm not coming back home," I lectured.

"Man, now a nigga got to wait and do it look like a nigga eat fruit? I rather eat yo ass then to eat this basic ass shit," his crazy self said making me laugh out loud while in the store.

"Man, bye I will see you in a little bit." I said immediately hanging up in his face while I laughed. I began to push my shopping cart and I ran directly into someone. My face wore a scowl as I looked up to see who would just be in my way. When our eyes met, my eyes bulged out of the sockets like frog eyes.

"Hmm damn, excuse me Heaven. Long time no see," Caleb smiled. Instead of it making my heart flutter like it used to, I was scared. I was not sure what to do. I was stuck. I had been ignoring this crazy ass nigga for a while. It's like we talk, he apologized, but when I told him I had to cut him off, his ass became more aggressive. He was calling and leaving threatening messages. He broke into my house and broke everything inside. When I say he destroyed it, he fucked my house up. I was so mad, but I wouldn't dare tell Ricardo because he warned me all bets was off if the nigga came anywhere near me again. Plus, I still had love for the nigga and didn't want to see him hurt. One thing I have learned, Ricardo was worse than his brother. He was logical, but he didn't believe in letting shit go. He always said the shit will always come back if you don't handle it right then and there.

"Um… Caleb… I…" I stuttered. I was falling apart. On the outside he looked normal, like his caring self when he was happy, but I knew the demon that laid on the inside of him. I knew I needed to get far away from him.

"Damn, it's no hard feelings Heaven. I see you have moved on. The house is bigger than mine, but nice. You got a new car too, I like it." He said coming closer to me and invading my space. This nigga is crazy as fuck. *How the hell do he know where I am staying and what car I am driving?* I thought to myself. This nigga is definitely not over it.

"One thing for sure Heaven, you can't get away from me. We belong together, just you wait baby." I could smell his minty breath. I was so scared to move. It was like I was stuck. He gently palmed my face and I wanted to run and scream, but the thought of this nigga chasing my ass down or showing up to Ricardo's home made me stay put. He bent down and pressed his lips against mine and held it there as if he were savoring it. He tried to part my lips with his tongue, but I would not allow it until he bite my bottom lip making me moan out in pain. He stuck his tongue in my mouth and the mixture of my blood and his saliva made me sick to my stomach. Finally, the feeling of guilt, disgust and violation made me pull away from him. I wiped my mouth with the back of my hand as the tears began to fall from my eyes.

"Still taste the same," he winked. He patted me on my butt making me jump, as he began to push his buggy and stroll down the aisle like nothing ever happened. I noticed a woman walk away and I swear she was recording us, but I could be wrong. I never seen her before, so I immediately walked away from the aisle and tried my best to gather my thoughts and grab the rest of the items I needed. I could not believe this nigga had the audacity to do some shit like this. I was so shaken up I paid the cashier and didn't even wait for my change. When I got to my car, I loaded all the groceries in the trunk and when I went to get inside the driver side of the car. There was a note attached to the steering wheel from Caleb. This nigga has taken stalker to a whole another level. There is no way this nigga could have broken in this car without a key. If he wanted to scare me, he did. I was so shaken up I could barely start the car. I was crying the whole drive to Kia's new home. I was so in a daze that at every damn red light I stopped at I was honked when it turned green. What the fuck was I going to do about this crazy ass nigga? He was not letting me go. As I got closer to Kia's home, I checked my rear-view mirror continuously to make sure I was not being followed. There is no way this nigga has not been following me if he knows where Ricardo stays and the fact I got a new car.

I finally pulled up at Kia's new home and sat outside for a few minutes while I gathered my thoughts. I admired the new home and truck Renzo got Kia as a push gift. I was happy for my cousin, but I really didn't want to bring this negative energy in her new home. I checked my surroundings making sure I didn't see anything out of the ordinary. I was just about to get out the car when I saw Renzo walking towards the house, but he was on FaceTime with a chick. I couldn't make out who it was, but I knew it definitely was not Kia. Kia had her hair in long straight back braids with blonde weave. I knew they were not in a relationship according to her and him, so for once I decided to mind the business that pays me. I got out the car and open the trunk. I guess Renzo heard my door and turned around to see who it was.

"Ima call you back," he said to the girl and hung up before she could respond. *Definitely is something if he doesn't want me to see it.* I thought to myself. "Damn, let me help you," Renzo stated jogging to me to help get the groceries out the car.

"Thanks," I tried to play it cool. We grabbed the bags, and I closed the trunk and hit the alarm as we walked up to the house, hearing a car pull up with speed and then stop made me turnaround quickly. Seeing it was the next-door neighbor, I turned around. Then the sound of an alarm made my body jump scared from the noise.

"Damn, you ok? You jumpy as hell," Renzo questioned with a curious look on his face. He then turned around and looked back on to the street.

"Um, yea I'm ok. The sound just scared me, didn't expect it," I lied through my teeth. I was paranoid as hell. He eyed me suspiciously before unlocking the door and letting me in the house first.

"Damn, took you long enough shit," Amber complained coming towards the door and grabbing some of the bags from me.

"Well, who told y'all to have a get together anyways?" I rolled my eyes.

"It was you and Kia's fat ass idea. Y'all love to eat." Amber complained again.

"You right," I dragged the word right and began to laugh. I went to the sink and washed my hands. Amber and I got started in the kitchen and began to get all the food prepared. We were making a soul food feast. Everyone was coming over, Auntie Sheila, who was Amber's mom, Auntie Ava which was Kia's mom and of course my mom as well. So, we wanted to be sure it was enough to go around. Kia had this new house laid. I had to refer her to someone since I had not started back working yet. I still had a few clients and referrals from past clients that I knew would need my assistance soon. I was just debating on what company I wanted to work under, but in the meantime, I was back taking classes.

"Damn, y'all got it smelling good in here," Chase came in the kitchen with a smile. He began to try and touch a piece of the fried chicken, but Amber's hand popped him so quick, he snatched back as soon as he felt the sting from the hit.

"Keep yo dirty hands to yourself. I know your ass didn't wash your hands," Amber chastised him. I laughed at the two as I stirred the pot with the greens.

"C'mon nigga before these girls beat yo ass about they food," Mack came in to rescue us from his greedy ass. The nigga could eat his ass off too. Chase was always the first person to get his plate at any gathering that involved food.

"Man, they trippin'. I just wanted to taste the damn chicken. Shit better be good the way y'all actin'," he frowned as he followed behind Mack, making me laugh.

"Girl, that man act like he hasn't ate in years," Karina said making herself known.

"Oh, shit it's you again?" Amber laughed.

"Right, he brought her around again. He must really like her," I mocked, making her blush.

"Hmmm something about that cougar," Amber joked making her fall out laughing. There was a small age difference between Karina and Chase by two years, but we loved to joke with her about it.

"Listen, I can't get the nigga to leave me alone or stop calling and it's only been a month," She dished some tea about her and Chase's situation.

"Shit enjoy it while you can, because these niggas fuck up on a daily," Kia walked in and said, making us turn around. She had a glow still about her and she carried our little cousin in her arms.

"Girl, I thought you was napping," I asked, putting the Pigeon peas and rice in a pan.

"Girl, this little nigga wants a breast in his mouth every damn thirty minutes," she rolled her eyes and sat on the barstool.

"You are giving him the best nutrients a mother could give," Karina smiled. "Can I hold him?" she asked, and Kia nodded her head yes. Karina excitedly ran to wash her hands and dry them before grabbing the baby. He stirred around from being passed to Karina, but after a few cooing noises he settled in her arms and had his eyes closed. I looked over at my little cousin and the little boy already had a Cuban bracelet and chain on. Like the boy was not even two months yet and had jewelry on.

"Damn, he so handsome," Karina stared at him in amazement.

"Thank you," Kia smiled as we all just stared at the little baby before us. The ringing of the doorbell took us out of our trance.

"I will get it," Kia stated as she walked to the door and after a few moments she opened the door. I could hear Ava soon as she walked through the door.

"Girl, what the fuck Renzo doing that got you laid up looking like this?" Ava shouted as she walked further inside the home. I instantly rolled my eyes because it was typical of her to do this. Like why you got to be so extra, just be happy for people and stop counting people's pockets.

"The same shit all your niggas did for you to live the way you did," Auntie Sheila said making us all laugh. We could hear them from the kitchen since they were so damn loud. I put the aluminum foil over the pans of food and exited the kitchen to see them all in the hallway of the house.

"Hello Ava," Kia dryly stated at her mother.

"Well, let us see this house," Auntie Sheila asked Kia, who looked slightly annoyed.

"C'mon and Ava don't ask me shit about nothing. Just be happy I'm paying your rent," Kia fussed trying to embarrass her mom. Their relationship was weird, but I could tell Kia was trying to be nice even though it was hard. I was shocked she was helping her mom, especially since she has not been there for her. I watched them follow behind Kia, and seeing my mom come close to me and smile.

"You ok Heaven?" my mother asked. She knew exactly when something was just not right with me.

"Yea ma, just a little tired from doing all this cooking," I partially told the truth.

"Hmm, ok if you need me, I'm here," she stared deeply in my eyes trying to read me.

"I will," I quickly advised, and walked away from her. She was making me nervous and honestly, a mother always knows when something isn't right, and my damn mama was good at it. I headed back into the kitchen to help put the finishing touches on the food. Amber was setting the dining room table.

"You need any help?" Karina asked.

"Yea, you can help me put the food in the serving bowls and pans," I advised her.

"Ok, let me give the baby back to Kia," she said before walking out of the kitchen. I continued what I was doing but something was definitely off. I had not spoken to Ricardo since I was in the store. It's like he heard my thoughts because the smell of his cologne hit me before he walked inside the kitchen. His eyebrows were furrowed, his body language gave off a rage, and his eyes were cold. I didn't understand why he looked so angry.

"Baby, What's wrong?" I asked him. He stared at me with his eyes looking like glaciers in the artic.

"So, what happened at the store?" he calmly asked, making the small hairs on my neck standup as fear swept me. He knew something, but how?

"I'm unsure what you are talking about?" I was completely nervous. My palms were sweaty, and my hands were shaky. I sat the spoon in the pot and walked towards him, hoping that I could calm him. I could see the fire igniting him.

"Yo, a nigga gon ask yo ass one more fucking time. What the fuck happened at the store?"

Ricardo bellowed making me jump back. Ricardo never yelled at me like this. This was a different type of anger.

"The fuck going on?" Renzo walked inside the kitchen looking at me and then Ricardo.

"A nigga trying to see what this hoe got going on now," Ricardo said, making my eyes open big and then a frown spread across it.

"Nigga, who the fuck is you calling a hoe! I don't even know what the fuck you are talking about," I yelled back. Before I could blink good, I could feel Ricardo's hand around my neck while he mushed the phone in my face of a picture I couldn't see fully.

"Bitch, ain't that's you kissing the nigga that beat your ass and tried to kill you!" he barked. My eyes blinked as I tried to breathe and finally through the tears, I could see the picture of me and Caleb's ass. Him kissing me and my ass just standing there.

"Yo Ric, she can't breathe," I could hear Renzo telling Ricardo, but his grip got tighter. I then could hear my cousins, aunties and mom yelling. Finally, feeling his grip loosen, I fell back on the floor trying to breathe. I could hear him yelling for the guys to let him go, but when I heard the last part before he walked out the door, my heart dropped in my ass. The words "I'm done," tore me up on the inside. I knew Ricardo was serious, but I didn't have an explanation. I just cried on the floor. I felt everyone surround me, but nothing could take away from this pain I felt. As much as I tried to fight it, I was completely in love with Ricardo and the fact he was done because I didn't have the heart to just tell him what happened to me immediately, I felt like I couldn't breathe. I began to hyperventilate.

"Heaven, breathe baby, breathe," my mother's voice in my ear soothed me. I could hear the commotion outside, but I couldn't make out what was being said. I sat there and just cried in my mother arms. Kia and Amber walked in the kitchen further.

"Kia, what happened? I'm so confused at what is going on?" I heard Amber asked.

"Heaven, the shit you just did is so fucked up. Why would you do that to Ric, like the nigga is fucked up about you," Kia sounded completely aggravated about my shenanigans.

"Heaven, what did you do?" My mother asked as she cradled me.

"Heaven, you do a lot of crazy shit, but after this shit, I can't even look at you. Why the fuck was you kissing Caleb in the grocery store not even three hours ago?" Kia's voice dripped with disgust.

"Your dumb ass did what now?" Amber's slick mouth ass said.

"That's not what happened," I tried to plead my case, but I could tell from the looks from around the room, everyone was thinking I was back with Caleb again.

"Well, talk then because Renzo outside now trying to keep Ricardo calm, so he won't come back in here trying to kill your simple self." The attitude that Kia displayed, made me feel like I had fucked up badly, even without me doing it on purpose.

"I ran into Caleb at the store. It's literally like he came out of nowhere. The nigga had like this crazy look in his eyes. He had been following me, there is no way he bumped into me by accident. He knew where I stayed at with Ricardo, he knew what car I was driving. I was scared he stepped so close to me and then he kissed me he made me feel so uncomfortable. I was scared he was going to do something crazy. I never told y'all, but the nigga broke into my house and broke everything in the house, like literally destroyed all my shit. Like I must replace everything. That's why I never pushed the issue of going back home. The nigga has lost his damn mind. The kiss that was captured in the picture had to come from when he kissed me before I could move away from him. I was nervous the nigga was going to drag my ass out of the damn store. Like whoever took that picture didn't stay to see what else happened..." I was in tears while I told them what happened, but when I realized the nigga got the picture from the pretty bitch in the aisle, I knew it was some shit between them, because I remember seeing the girl and wondering why she was the only one in the aisle and she literally watched the uncomfortable ordeal. I jumped up quickly with my anger rising. "Oh, this nigga got me fucked up!" I shouted pushing past everyone to get outside. The minute I saw him I took off in his direction. Mack grabbed me by my waist realizing I was on attack mode.

"Nigga, you got some nerve the brown bitch in the grocery aisle is the one who sent you the picture huh! The bitch couldn't wait to show your ass, but she forgot to tell you the whole fucking truth! You didn't let me explain shit but let this bitch who you probably fucking on a daily tell you about me! fuck you!" I spat.

"At least she realer than you. She would have told me from the jump what happened. Man a nigga ain't got time for your secretive ass anyways. I rather fuck ten bitches then to deal with a sneaky ass liar! Man, go let yo ex continue knocking your fucking brain loose and teeth out your mouth so you can keep getting them shits fixed!" he barked, turning around. I got so mad, I escaped out of Mack's grip and took one of the heavy stones from around the garden bed of flowers and ran towards his car and smashed the front window with it. I was moving too fast for Mack to catch me and plus he had to help restrain Ric. I ran in the house, with my cousins, Momma, and aunties behind me trying to talk some sense into me, but I heard nothing. My feelings were hurt. I was mad at myself for not even telling him upfront what happened, but I also was mad at him for not just hearing me out. I was even more mad because the nigga had a whole bitch he was fucking on the side, because ain't no friend snitching and not making it known right then and there as the situation occurred. I grabbed a big ass knife from out of the drawer and when I turned around to head back out the door, everyone parted like the red sea when they saw me.

"Oh, this nigga got me fucked up. All this shit I been through, he wants to fuck bitches and shit! I got my ass beat to be with his stupid ass," I talked out loud to myself.

"The bitch done lost it. She talking to herself," I heard Ava say, when I appeared outside and headed for his whip, Ricardo must have become the fucking hulk. The nigga found his way to me before I could slash all his fucking tires. The way my body snatched back, and the knife dropped out of my hand I began kicking and screaming! I felt my body hit the hard ground with the grass saving me from a hard fall.

"You want to fuck my shit up because you got caught on some shit. I told you Heaven to dead that shit, and you didn't so leave me the fuck alone, I'm done!" he yelled at me. With every word at that moment, I knew exactly who I was in love with. Every word broke my heart into pieces. My anger turned into begging.

"No, no, no, please it's not what it looks like," I cried as I tried to hold on to him. He was on top of me trying to get up, but I held on to his shirt and grabbed his arm while he tried to pull away. He facial expression showed nothing but hurt and disgust. "Please, Ric I'm sorry baby. I'm sorry! It's not what you think!" I pleaded with tears in my eyes. I continued to try and hold on to him, but he became more aggressive trying to get me to not touch him. When he finally got up, I quickly did too and chased behind him. I couldn't help it I was hurt and distraught. I didn't care how I looked I just knew I couldn't lose the one person who was here for me through it all. "Please Ric just listen," I cried like a big baby. He looked me over one good time and shook his head.

"Yo Renzo, I'm going to send someone over here to fix the window. I will have Chase bring the car back," he spoke to Renzo who nodded his head. I saw Chase walking towards the whip because he knew he had to drop Ric off. I began to walk towards the car quickly, but my sobbing was slowing me down because I could barely breathe.

"Please, Ric just talk to me," I was barely able to get out.

"Chase, hurry the fuck up!" He snapped and his eyes were cold as he mugged me, making me stay put. When the doors closed to my car and he drove off, I broke down in the front yard. Just like that, Caleb broke us up and I was not even messing with the nigga. This was the worst break up I ever felt, now I knew how it felt to lose a real nigga.

CRAZY ATTRACTION

Kia

After finally getting Heaven to calm down, I went to check on my son and noticed the bedroom window was open. Walking over to the crib he was laying sound asleep, but this uneasy feeling came over me. I went to the window examining the windowsill and then looking on the outside and I could have sworn I seen someone staring off in the distance, but since it was dark now, I wasn't sure at what I was fucking looking at. I closed the window and put the latch on it to make sure it was secured. I went and picked my little man up and held him in my arms and planted a kiss on his forehead. I walked out the room holding him and headed into the den. I sat on the couch and laid my son on my chest.

"Girl, if you don't stop spoiling him, he won't let no one watch him," Ava complained.

"Well, I definitely won't leave him with you," I rolled my eyes.

"Karina! You want a plate because I'm packing food to go since these niggas want to fight bitches and shit!" Chases greedy ass yelled from the kitchen.

"Yea, let me go tend to this crazy boy before he says something else stupid," Karina said getting up from the couch and quickly leaving to tend to Chase. Renzo walked in and sat next to me. He looked worried.

"You good?" I asked him and he nodded his head yes and snuggled next to me and the baby. Even though we were not together, Renzo put the baby and me first. I noticed his phone ringing and I was trying so hard to see the caller ID, but once I notice it was just a number, I got irritated because he silenced the phone. So, whoever it was, I was not going to know or see.

"I packed everyone to go plates since today was a bit much," Amber came in the den area.

"Definitely was. You think Heaven will be ok?" My Auntie Sheila asked. She was sincere and we were all worried. The last time a nigga broke her heart, she went into a bad depression, and honestly, I don't think she expected to fall for Ricardo so this just might make it worst for her.

"Not sure, but she is laying down, and I will let her stay here until she is ready to go back home," I told my aunts and mother.

"One thing for sure, a nigga either can make you the happiest person in the world or make you so sad that you can't function properly," Auntie Sheila spoke from experience the way her voice conveyed the statement.

"Damn, right. I remember when I first caught Kia's daddy cheating on me. I was dumb founded that I cried for a week straight," my mother reminisced.

"Yep, and then after that the nigga tried to kill you, because you decided to pretend you was talking to the nigga Roland from around the corner," Auntie Kissa said with laughter, who is Heaven's mother.

"Oh, shit I remember that. His ass didn't play no more after that. Couldn't pay Kia's daddy to even look at a girl," Auntie Sheila laughed, making everyone else laugh too.

"Girl, your daddy was my everything," she smiled at the thought.

"Clearly, he got the best of you, while I didn't," I sarcastically spoke before I got up with my son in my arms and walking into the kitchen. I was still sensitive about my mother and all the shit she put me through. The shit just never went away no matter how hard I tried. I walked inside the kitchen and saw Karina and Chase being frisky in the corner and Mack was in his phone.

"Yo, Kia cut her some slack she trying," Renzo came in the kitchen behind me to say.

"Yea well don't reminisce on some shit after you said fuck your daughter. Let's not bring up the past anymore. It hurts for me still," I expressed. For some reason after having this baby my emotions have been up and down. I read about postpartum, but I honestly felt like I was feeling it a lot more lately.

"Look, just relax aiight. I'm going to slide. I will come back later tonight," he advised me.

"For what? It's already late," I instantly got an attitude.

"Chill shawty, a nigga got shit to do, and I got a little nigga to take care of," he simply stated.

"Yea, but you need to be safe too," I expressed.

"Just relax and I will see you later," he came close to me and kissed my son forehead and then kissed mine. I was so aggravated at the fact he was leaving.

"Chase, we got moves to make," Renzo told him before he left out the door.

"Aiight, c'mon girl. I got to get some pussy and eat before I make moves," Chase's silly ass said.

"Boy!" Karina yelled and popped Chase upside the head. "Just embarrassing" Karina said making me laugh.

"Thank you for coming girl," I said to Karina, and she gave me a hug.

"It was a pleasure, and your home is everything," she sweetly spoke.

"Thank you, make it home safe," I said as I walked them out and locked the door behind them. I walked back into the den area and noticed everyone was talking and laughing. I then walked to the back to check on Heaven. Peeping inside the room I could see her still sleeping. I headed back to the den area where I saw my aunts and mother getting to up to leave. I was sort of relieved because I had enough of company and drama for one day.

"Thanks for the invite. Take care of my baby," Aunty Kissa said to me after she gave me a hug.

"I will, I promise," I assured her before watching them walk out the door and head to the car. Once the headlights cut on and the car backed up out of my driveway, I closed the door and locked it. I walked back to the den, where Amber was comfortably laid out under the blanket.

"You not going home?" I asked her and she shook her head no. "Well, here watch your little cousin, I need to shower." I told her, laying him on her chest. He squirmed a little but never opened his bright eyes. I went to my bedroom and got in the shower. I was enjoying the hot water as it hit my body. *Damn, I needed this,* I thought to myself. After a about thirty minutes, I was out of the shower and in my bedroom rubbing body butter all over my body. I then put on my silk short set pajamas and wrapped my scarf around my head. I headed to check on Heaven, but she wasn't in the guest room. I found her in the den with Amber. Her eyes were puffy and red. She looked completely distraught.

"You good Heaven?" I asked her as I grabbed my baby from Amber.

"I mean no. Ricardo is not answering my calls. He won't let me explain," she sighed deeply.

"Give him some time to think and process what he saw," I advised her. I honestly didn't think she had a chance in hell because Ricardo was very no nonsense when it came to shit. Certain shit just wouldn't move him.

"I don't think he is Kia. I swear I didn't kiss Caleb, he kissed me. I was crying and scared. I pulled away from him like the picture of us don't even look like I was even enjoying it," Heaven expressed. I felt bad for my cousin because if what she said was true, Caleb needs his ass beat, but I knew the soft ass girl wasn't going to let the boys do anything and I think that's what irritated Ricardo more It wasn't that she kissed him, or he kissed her. It's the fact he won't be able to touch the nigga for the disrespect.

"Look, you either let them check this nigga or you deal with the bullshit ahead, but I'm here to tell you nothing good is coming out of this shit. If you keep quiet about all the shit he has been doing." I truthfully told her. The nigga was walking around like he was untouchable and honestly needed to be handled.

"What I'm supposed to do? Have them kill the nigga?" her dumb ass said. I looked at this girl as if she had two heads.

"So, you mean to tell me it was ok for the nigga to beat your ass till you was in the hospital and then try to kill your ass again afterwards. Now he gets to walk around like ain't shit happened and live his damn life." I made known to Heaven as I looked at her in disbelief. This was not ok or normal. *Yep, this girl is definitely brain dead,* I thought to myself.

"Girl you sound like some kind of stupid. When did you become so gullible? I think that nigga made your brain turn into mush," Amber was laid on the couch in her phone with her nose turned up in a frown.

"Well, excuse me I'm not allowed to be dumb for a nigga, but y'all two can? Real funny how y'all have so much to say about me, but I have watched you become a sister wife, and you fight bitches everyday over a nigga who didn't have the decency to not fuck bitches that were too close to your place of residence and business." Heaven tried to check us, but she had the right one today.

"You damn right I fought bitches and handled up on Renzo's ass too, but I have never been dumb enough to let a nigga beat my ass until I was unconscious or the fact you had to get new teeth because he knocked your shit out! I may have put up with hoes, but no nigga will ever beat my ass and I go back multiple times to get my ass handed to me every single time. I rather be able to fight a bitch fair and square then to be laid up in a hospital bed over a nigga who only care if I'm alive just so I won't tell the police what happened. You're fucking nuts and got some nerve. Get your shit and get the fuck out my house talking shit. My cheating ass baby daddy paid for it and his brother took care of your simple ass when that nigga took everything from you!" I snapped. I was so mad I got up and walked out the den and headed into the kitchen. This bitch had lost her mind talking to me sideways.

"Hmph, she told your stupid ass. Look who's doing dumb shit now. Losing a good man!" I heard Amber taunt her. I smirked because this bitch just wanted to say something, but I had said a mouthful so there wasn't much to say. After a few minutes I heard my front door open and slam hard. I felt bad for making her leave, but the girl's mouth could be so disrespectful. My alarm was blaring through the house. I heard a few buttons press on the keypad from Amber turning the alarm off and then back on. I heard her lock the door and walk in the kitchen where I was standing.

"Girl, I'm going to sleep. I'm happy she is gone. I didn't want to share a bed with her ass anyways," Amber laughed. I couldn't do nothing but shake my damn head tonight had to be one for the books, because something was always going down when we all got together for a good time. I got the baby ready for bed and soon as we laid down, my eyes were closed and met with darkness and the sleep took over.

Waking up and realizing my son was not next to me I began to panic. I jumped up from the bed running towards his room. Noticing it was empty I quickly walked towards the den area seeing Renzo with the baby on his chest with his eyes closed made me put my hand over my chest in relief. I took a deep breath trying to get my breathing in order. I heard movement in the kitchen. I walked in seeing Amber fixing herself a cup of coffee, looking all dolled for work made me realized I had a doctor's appointment this morning.

"Shit!" Amber yelped and dropped her phone, while holding her chest. "Girl the hell you creeping up on me for? You scared me." She took a deep breath and sat the cup on the counter and lean down to the ground to grab her phone.

"My bad, you headed to work?" I asked the question I already knew the answer to.

"Girl, yes because Mack's ass been trying to find ways to keep a bitch busy. He won't let me be a great person and live my damn life."

"Well, I have a doctor's appointment this morning so let me hurry up and get myself together. You coming back over?" I questioned her. I hated being home alone, ever since the incident with Nadia. I was scared the bitch was out there just waiting.

"No, I'm going home I have some work that I need to finish and plus I need to help your stupid ass cousin try and get her nigga back. The bitch ruined her damn birthday." She rolled her eyes in annoyance.

"I heard it was going to be big, and he went all out." I remembered Renzo pillow talking about it.

"Yes, like bitch everything is done and paid for. He's just refusing to go or speak to her. I talked to him this morning and if I didn't know any better the nigga sounded like he was around a bitch because the hoe yawned loud as fuck in the background," Amber dished some tea out to me, with the you didn't hear this from me look.

"Damn he just like his fucking brother a damn hoe!" I turned my nose up in disgust.

"They niggas. They get hurt bitch; they can never take that shit. Niggas talk all that shit but let a bitch hurt them, they have that hurt hoe syndrome. Where they have to try and one up your already one up," Amber's silly ass said. Her logic always sounded crazy as hell.

"Girl you are crazy," I laughed.

"No, these niggas are for thinking they slicker than us," she giggled. She grabbed her purse and laptop bag along with her coffee. "Call you later to check on y'all," she gave me kiss on the cheek.

"Girl don't be kissing me. I don't know where your mouth been," I rubbed my cheek as I pretended to be so disgusted.

"Girl bye, the same where yours been," she yelled at me as she headed for the door. I heard her turn the alarm off as she opened the door and walked outside. I was right behind her to lock it. I put the alarm back on and headed to get dress, because I didn't want to be late to my appointment. I went inside the bathroom and took a shower. I then brushed and rinsed my mouth out with the Listerine. I walked out of the bathroom and into my room, I jumped at the sight of Renzo laid on the bed with our son. He looked up at me and smirked.

"Nigga, you scared the fuck out of me," I put my hand over my chest.

"Your ass always jumpy," he looked down at his phone.

"Um, can you get out while I get dressed?" I tried to grab my towel and cover myself.

"Man, girl a nigga done seen everything you had to offer already. I literally know you inside and out," He laughed.

"Shut the hell up!" I rolled my eyes and wrapped the towel fully around me. I went to my closet and grabbed some high waisted jeans, a graphic tee shirt, and then my panties and bra from the drawer. I went back inside the bathroom and got dressed. I had to admit the baby left me even thicker. My ass was fat, and my thighs were big.

My legs were even thick, making it hard to pull the skinny jeans up my legs. My waist was almost back to its normal size, but I knew I would need to work out since I still had a small pudge. For the most part, me changing my diet and keeping my stomach wrapped helped a lot. I grabbed my Louis Vuitton sandals, matching belt and bag. I had to admit there was perks being Renzo's baby mama. The nigga gave me all types of push gifts when I got out the hospital. I just wished he would have just given me all of him instead. I rubbed some of the Jimmy Choo lotion on my arms and neck and then sprayed those same areas and all over my body. I took my scarf off my head and then relayed my baby hairs. I then put on my simple studded earrings and diamond cross necklace. I glossed my lips and filled my eyebrows and used the concealer on them to look as natural as possible, since they were a little thick and unruly.

"Damn, you fine as fuck," Renzo said looking at me from head to toe. I instantly became uncomfortably shy. I fidgeted a little and had a smile on my face.

"You think so? I feel a little stuffed," I truthfully responded.

"I mean, shit one fine ass stuffed chicken," this stupid nigga said making me burst into laughter. "Where the hell you going?" he curiously asked.

"Well, I was headed to the doctor," I told him as I was grabbing my phone and keys.

"Aww hell naw. I'm coming too," he jumped up going into the bathroom.

"Wait what, but we going to be late if we have to take the baby," I whined.

"Man, get my little nigga ready and if you stop the whining and just start moving you won't be late," he fussed at me. Getting annoyed, I just did as I was told and got the baby bag together as well as got the baby ready to go. After an additional fifteen minutes, we were on our way out the door.

Renzo drove while I sat in the back with the baby. I had to admit with all the shit I been through, this baby always slept unless he was hungry. I was so sure I was going to have a crybaby because my pregnancy was the worse. I knew by the time we made it to doctor's office it would be time to feed him again, since I fed him not to long ago. While driving to the doctor's I notice Renzo kept looking in the rearview mirror.

"Yo, Kia can you see who in that truck behind us?" he asked. I looked back and the front window shield was tinted dark so I couldn't see inside. The truck gave off DT vibes.

"You got anything in the whip?" I asked him.

"Naw, but the shit look like it's following me," his voice expressed worry.

"I mean it looks like DT and if that's them, if they pull us over oh well, everything we have is good," I reassured him.

"You right, but I don't think that's DT man. The shit just looks fucking weird. DT don't follow behind you this long and not pull you," he said something that was definitely true. "I'm going to turn here and if they follow behind us pull your gun out," he advised. Since I was license to carry, I had my gun on me at all times when we drove around with the baby in the car. He made a right turn and we pulled to the side and waited for the truck to turn, but I noticed it passed by never making the right turn behind us. We both took a sigh in relief.

"That was weird as hell," Renzo expressed.

"Let me ask you, what ever happened to Nadia?" I was curious because this was a subject that have not been brought up since his last visit to see Lolita. The last time I checked they didn't know where her ass was then.

"Honestly, a nigga don't know. I tried on my own to find her, but I got nothing. Lolita said the bitch was never going to be a bother, but they don't even know where she is." What he said sent my nerves into a frenzy. This bitch had to be out there just lurking. I got what she wants, and I don't believe she would stop until she got it.

"Renzo the fuck you mean you don't know?The bitch is delusional," I snapped.

"Look, you are safe, and Lolita promised me that we were good and if anything happens, she knows how shit going to go down, so just chill and trust I got you," he firmly spoke.

"This shit your fault. We have a son to think about now. You should have kept your fucking dick in your pants. Like out of all the bitches you always got to fuck the hoes that's close to me," I was aggravated and scared. Say what you want, but the bitch Nadia was fucking crazy and there was no telling what the fuck she had going on.

"Man, kill that shit. A nigga don't need no reminders of shit. If shit happens, a bitch gon die that's it," he said as he glanced in the rearview mirror at me. I rolled my eyes because the shit he was talking went in one ear and out the other. Say what you want sometimes a person with a broken heart was far worse than anyone. He continued the drive to the doctor's office, which we made it there in about fifteen minutes. The car ride was quiet even down to us making it into the doctor's office. I didn't have anything to say to him. We sat in the waiting room waiting for my name to be called. I was holding my son and breast feeding while we waited. I was super annoyed with Renzo and lowkey mad he was there with me. His phone started vibrating loudly in his pocket. He pulled it out and a phone number came across the screen that I did not recognize. He looked at the phone for a few seconds before he looked at me, I rolled my eyes because I knew it had to be a bitch if the nigga didn't want to answer it and was looking at me to see my expression. He got up and answered the phone right before walking out the door. I just knew it was a bitch, but shit what could I do or say? I made it truly clear we were just co-parenting.

By the time he came back inside from being on the phone, my name was called. I had already stopped feeding the baby and was preparing to give him the baby so I could go to the back. He motioned for me to put him in the carrier car seat that sat in the chair next to us. He then grabbed the baby bag and the carrier with the baby inside and tried to follow me to the back.

"Um, what are you doing?" I asked him and he looked at me as if I was crazy.

"A nigga needs to see what's going on with your pussy too. You almost lost a uterus," he seriously said making me turn beet red as I looked around at everyone now staring at me. The nigga walked past me and headed inside the office with nurse looking at me with a smirk. She had gotten use to Renzo's behavior. I rolled my eyes at her, and she fell out laughing as I walked past her, and she let the door close.

"You two are in room five. Remove your clothes and sit on the table. Are you still bleeding?" she asked, and I shook my head no. "Ok, good we will knock before coming in," she stated, and we walked into to room 5 and closed the door.

"Renzo you need to learn to respect my privacy. We have a child together, but we are not together," I said in frustration as I took my clothes off to put on the paper material and sit on the fake ass bed, they had on one side of the room.

"Man shut that shit up. A nigga trying to make sure the shit ain't broken," he waived me off as he sat in the chair next to the bed and placed the baby directly in front of him on the floor as he slept in his carrier.

"Don't you got a whole chick you talking to? Why do you care if my shit broken or not?" I snapped.

"I do, but we ain't fucking yet, so if I can hit your shit and talk to her on the phone, I'm good," he truthfully said making me lean over smacking his ass upside the head.

"Nigga you just don't care what the fuck you say." My feelings were hurt to actually hear him tell me the truth.

"What? I'm never lying again so if you don't like my honesty Kia, then I'm unsure what to tell you," He spoke honestly, and I laid back on the table and just ignored his comment. I was so sure I was done with Renzo, but then he does things for me that makes me think otherwise. The doctor knocked and then walked inside.

"Well, hello Kia. How are you feeling today?" My nurse practitioner said to me. The middle-aged woman was always super nice to me.

"Ms. Donna, I feel good just adjusting to being a mom," I truthfully told her.

"Well, that's good. Let me just exam your uterus and make sure you're healing properly," she said, and I nodded my head in agreement. She called the assisting nurse inside and she did the examination.

"Well, it looks like you could have some scar tissue, but I want to do a sonogram to be sure, but everything looks good. Looks like dad made the right decision not allowing them to do the hysterectomy." She smiled at Renzo.

"Well, will she be able to have kids still?" Renzo asked and my eyes popped out the socket. The hell this nigga asking that for.

"Well, depending on the scar tissue anything is possible, but she might be a high risk due to how this first pregnancy went for her," She explained.

"Well, there is no need to worry about that. I am done having kids," I told her but was more so letting Renzo know too.

"Yea aiight, so can she have sex now?" Renzo's silly ass asked my doctor making me cover my face in embarrassment and she laughed.

"Well, yep she is in the clear, but she is definitely more fertile at this time, so do you want any contraceptives?" she asked me.

"Yes please, preferably non hormonal birth controls." I advised.

"Good, I will write a prescription for you, and your appointment will be scheduled for your sonogram as well. Everything will be ready for you at check out. Any questions?" she asked, and I shook my head no. "Great see you at your next visit," she said before walking out the door. I got up and wiped my vagina clean from the lubrication she used. I then put my clothes on.

"You shouldn't take the birth control. It's not healthy for you," Renzo said handing me my purse and the baby bag.

"Listen, Renzo we good and all, but my vagina care is my business and not yours so do me a favor let this be your last time coming with me to the doctor," I advised him, and he gave me this look as if I was speaking another language.

"Kill that shit there. Everything about you is my business, especially if you're my son's mother," he firmly stated and walked out the room while holding the carrier with the baby in it. I rolled my eyes to the ceiling and followed behind him.

Once I got my prescription and my appointment set, we left out of the doctor's office. We ended up going out to eat for lunch. I wasn't expecting it, but I wasn't about to argue about food. Once we walked inside Shooters, we were seated, and we had the baby car seat in the chair. Renzo had his son facing him. He was completely in love with this baby. I sat quietly until the waitress came and took our orders. I was in my feelings about everything. I think I needed to stop spending so much time with Renzo. I think he was lowkey wearing me down. His phone rang and he answered.

I could tell he was talking to Ricardo because of what they were speaking about. I grabbed my phone and started scrolling through social media, while I waited for him to finish.

"Nigga, why you can't come to the party that you throwing for the damn girl?" Renzo's statement piqued my interest as I now began to pay the conversation attention.

"Nigga you didn't go home?" Renzo asked.

"Aiight now don't end up in no shit because it was flaw of her to send that shit to you anyways. If you ask me the hoe being messy and that's a sign right there to leave that shit there," Renzo stated but I could tell from the look on his face he forgot I was sitting in front of him that quick.

"Look, I will meet you later. We got some shit to handle anyways," he advised to Ricardo on the call before they disconnected the line.

"Don't ask me shit you know I'm not going to do," I said before he could even ask me to keep his little conversation a secret, because that was not happening. He shrugged his shoulders, and we enjoyed our lunch together because there was nothing further to discuss after that. I just couldn't wait to spill my little tea to Heaven because if we could find this little broad who fucked her shit up, we could beat this little bitch's ass for not minding her business.

TAKE AWAY THE PAIN

Amber

The day came for Heaven's surprise
birthday party. I had to admit Ricardo went all out
for Heaven. He rented a nice ass venue and had it
decorated in all white with a beige accent color. He
requested for us to only provide him the numbers to
the vendors to make the party a hit and all we had to
do was the guest list. He made the calls and made
the payments to make this party happen. When you
walked in, it seems like you were stepping into
another world. It was extravagant. Heaven knew a
lot of people, so it wasn't hard putting her guess list
together with Kia's help. Her gift table had all types
of designer gift bags and presents in wrapped boxes.
Friends and family poured into the building to
celebrate for her or was just here for the free food
and liquor. Even though we knew Heaven was
going to be super excited and happy, the bad part in
all this was getting Ricardo to come. He was dead

set on not coming but wanted us to ensure she had a good time. It was already hard enough to get her to come out for her birthday since the nigga been ignoring her. She even got so mad; she went back home. I felt so bad for my cousin, but she kind of created the shit hole she was in.

I looked around and notice a lot of the guy's friends was here. They bought all the niggas out and they were fine too. I was hoping I got lucky, and they didn't know Mack's simple ass. I was dressed in an all-white knee length fitted dress that exposed my full back and had a deep plunge in the front exposing my 36 B cup breast. I wore a nude YSL heel, with a nude YSL bag to match. I walked around mingling until I saw Kia walked through the door looking like a whole lot of damn money. Her jewels glistened in the low lighting and her outfit made all heads turn. She was dressed in all white. Her top part of the dress was lace with thick material to cover her breast nipples and everything else was sheer. The bottom part of the dress was sheer and glistened with crystal like material. The dress exposed the white panty like bottom she had on. I couldn't believe Renzo let her out the house like that. Her ass cheeks were on full display and since sis had the baby, she was thicker than a snicker. Kia had hips, ass and legs for days. She wore nude red bottoms and a small YSL nude purse. Her makeup was flawless, and she had her hair in a sew-in that was long and straight. I think the fact her hair was burgundy gave her so much attention. I watched her began to walk directly over to me.

"Girl, you know it was a hassle to get this crazy girl to come here," she seemed flustered.

"Well, where is she?" I asked not seeing her walk in.

"She is almost here so get everyone ready," she advised me. While she walked back out the door, I got on the mic to get everyone to settle down and be prepared to say surprise. After about ten minutes of us getting everyone settled and her arriving, you could hear her fussing with Kia as they walked inside. The minute her face entered through the curtains, and we all yelled surprise her face of shock was everything. The tears began to form, while we tried to get her under control so she wouldn't ruin her makeup. She was shocked and happy. I had to admit birthday girl was looking damn good in the nude and white body suit that had sheer parts running up and down her body, letting us know she didn't have on any underclothing.

"Oh my God, thank you so much," Heaven continuously said as we tried to dry her eyes. All the boys came and gave her a hug, but the one person she wanted wasn't there. You could see the solemn look on her face even as she interacted with everyone. While all the guests were finally on the dance floor and the party was in full swing, I found Heaven at her designated area picking over the food.

"You ok?" I asked her, placing my hand on her shoulder.

"I mean, I'm grateful but I want my nigga back," she said in defeat.

"Look, don't worry he will come around. Shit he did all this for you," I tried to assure her, but shit even I wasn't convinced my damn self that the nigga was coming back. He was being so mean, but then again, he was making sure he kept his word on all the shit he did have previously planned.

"Easy for you to say, but you don't even believe that shit," She honestly said.

"Look, c'mon let's go to the dance floor. It's your birthday and plus you got some raw as gifts my girl," I tried to cheer her up. She smiled slightly and got up from the table. I took her by her gifts and her eyes was in awe at all the shit she got. "C'mon let's go dance I told her," Pulling her away before her ass noticed damn near half of the gifts came from Ricardo and she begins this sad shit again. We were on the dance floor cutting up. As the DJ played all the Miami music that had us stickin' and rolling, you couldn't tell us nothing. When the DJ started playing reggae it was over. The way Heaven was winding her hips to the beat and making her booty pop all eyes were on her as the crowd went crazy. Sis long 32-inch curls were bouncing everywhere as everyone cheered her on. This night was epic. Kia started moving her hips sensually as she came closer to Heaven. People didn't know, but Kia was a dancer. The way she started ticking her lower part of her body making her booty jiggle every time she made her body tick to the beat, I just knew Renzo was going to pop out of nowhere. The nigga didn't pull up yet, but when he did see Kia, he was going to lose his shit. Kia was cutting up on the dance floor. I made sure to film everything for memories. When the DJ played Young Dolph, I just knew these hoes were going to start shaking they ass. The beat dropped for Young Dolph's *Get Paid*. I watched Kia turn into a whole thug the way she rapped his lyrics loud as hell.

That bitch good as tooken, good as gone
I guarantee tonight my nigga, that bitch ain't
coming home
I got money to count, I got bitches to fuck.
I got packs to flip, pistols to bust.
When I was small, I ain't have nothing.
Started selling dope and prayed to God for a
plug.

He showed up and said

Kia was pointing her finger to the sky and when the hook dropped, she was shaking her ass on Heaven as they yelled the lyrics together.

Get paid, young nigga, get paid.
Get paid, young nigga, get paid.
Get paid, young nigga, get paid!
Whatever you do, just make sure you get paid.

They had everyone on the vibes. This party was amazing. Everyone interacted and was on the dance floor. You barely saw people sitting down unless they were resting. The food and drinks were amazing. There was two hookahs per table. Like I admired the décor and how it exemplifies simplicity and extravagance, which is Heaven's character. I finally walked away and headed to the bar. I wanted me a shot of Casamigos. When I felt a presence behind me, I turned around and saw Troy and he didn't have a crutch in sight.

"Well, damn handsome you have made a grand entrance," I gushed over in excitement and immediately hugged him. We were wrapped up in our own world for a few before he let me go.

"Damn, it's good seeing you. A nigga really misses your crazy ass," he smiled.

"Same here. Is that your date," I asked him, while gesturing to the broad that had her eyes glued to us. He turned around and notice the girl.

"Yea, that is my ex-fiancée," he smirked.

"Well tell sis I can fight, but I definitely don't want you," I laughed. If she knew better, she would do better, because if I wanted her nigga, I could have him.

"You say that now, but I'm gon let you do you, but you know where it's at," he planted a kiss on my cheek with his thick full lips. Troy's fine ass could get it any day, but just not today. I was going to do a mental note and pull up on that nigga one of these days. I was single and it didn't hurt to mingle. I watched him walk away towards the girl who was visibly mad, but whatever he said to her, she tightened her attitude the fuck up. I took my shot to the head that the bartender placed on the bar and walked away when I ran smack into Mack's ass.

"Damn nigga you almost knocked me down," I snapped, rubbing my hands down my dress as if he messed it up.

"Amber, a nigga needs to talk to you," he expressed but I was done talking. Even though Mack was always invading my space, I gave him little to none of the conversation he really wanted to have. Today was just another day where I was going to send his ass on with that bullshit. I didn't want to discuss shit if Tina was still having this damn baby.

"Mack, I told you multiple times no and this is definitely not the time and place. We are not together so the quicker you move on; the better life would be for you."

"A nigga just need you to listen for two minutes," he pleaded. I looked up at him and I'm not going to lie, I miss what we had but the fact still remain he had a child on the way and had me playing sister wives and shit.

"No," I dryly stated and walked off. I was over it and right now was not the time. I saw Ricardo walk in and I was so happy. I swiftly moved through the crowded people to get to him. He was dressed in all black and I had to admit the nigga cleaned up well. He had on diamond cuff links and his suit was accented with the same beige in Heaven's dress. His shoes were a beige Versace oxford shoes with the gold accent on them. His jewelry wasn't to much as he only had on one Cuban link necklace with another small chain that laid on his chest. He wore a Cuban bracelet and an all-diamond bracelet, along with a simple Hublot watch. I knew he paid a fortune because I remember Heaven fussing with him about his expensive watch collection. Sis was mad about that purchase because she said she could have just bought an investment property with the money he spent on that watch. One thing I learned about Ricardo was the nigga was smart and far richer than his brother and friend.

"You made it," I excitedly expressed.

"Yea, after your last message about coming to tear all my shit up in the house, I just came. I don't got time for you three to be breaking my shit," he honestly said. I chuckled at the thought of him taking heed to my threats.

"Look she will be super happy to see you. You know she loves you right?" I asked.

"A nigga knows that, but she needs to know keeping shit and not saying shit when it happens is a no go. I can't get with that sneaky ass shit," he firmly said. From the way he was talking I could tell he wasn't feeling her still.

"Let me ask you, do you believe the kiss was more on her or him?" I questioned.

"Honestly, in the picture I could see the tears. I knew it wasn't her choice, but she won't let me handle the nigga, so I just rather not deal with her, because the more attached I become, I can't promise I'm going to be civil with the nigga. I just want to beat the niggas ass that's it."

"I feel you, me and you both," I said in agreeance with him. We stood there for a few while he observed everyone. When his eyes laid on Heaven, I could tell he was amused at her dancing with Kia still. The music had shifted to that old Silk, and I watched Ricardo walk off to meet her on the dancefloor. I was right behind him recording. Her face when she saw him was instantly stained with tears. He smiled big as he tried to wipe them away, landing a kiss on her lips. I captured the best moment on picture as everyone grabbed a dance partner and started slow grinding, I took pictures and hyped people up while doing so. I saw Renzo come in and when his eyes landed on Kia dancing with some nigga, I just knew all hell was going to bust wide open. Renzo had this look in his eyes, but I could tell he was trying to stay calm. When he made it to Kia, the nigga quickly took one look at Renzo and backed off. The face Kia wore in annoyance had me crying out laughing. I just knew Renzo was going to jack her ass up, but he didn't. He whispered something in her ear and next thing I know he pop kissed her in the mouth and spun her around so that her ass was in front of him and pulled her in and they slow grinded on the floor as she had a big smile on her face. This was the first time ever our family had all smiles. I was super happy about that.

I finally sat down at the table and had one of the waiters to bring me a plate of food. I scrolled through my phone a little. I felt a presence over me, and I saw it was Heaven all smiles.

"You guys did your thang," she slurred slightly. She was fucked up.

"Girl anything for you Ms. Prissy," I teased.

"Girl, I think my feet on fire now from all that dancing. Did I sweat my makeup off?" Kia whined.

"No girl," I said to her.

"Why you sitting down here?" Kia questioned.

"Girl, waiting for them to bring me some food," I said to Kia.

"Nope her ass is sad about Mack and Troy bought his little girlfriend with him." Heaven's drunk ass said.

"Heaven, why the girlfriend got to be little?" Kia asked.

"Because her ass is, looking like a whole little boy; no shape, just skinny. Everything little on her, even her lips," Heaven's statement made scream in laughter.

"Bitch you stupid," Kia laughed as well. I could always count on them to make me laugh when I needed it. Heaven stood up and was in front of me dancing to some City Girl's song, but when this nigga had the audacity to roll up on her I couldn't even believe my eyes. How the hell did he get past the guys? Caleb grabbed Heave from behind. I was so stuck because I was in shock that he was bold enough to show up here. Heaven turned around quickly thinking it was Ricardo, but when she was met with Caleb's face instead, she backed up quickly.

"The fuck you doing here?" Heaven snapped. Thank God the music was loud because no one notice the commotion that was brewing.

"Damn, baby I told you I was coming for you. I miss you," he tried to reach for Heaven again, but she pulled away.

"Yo Caleb, this not the time or place," I firmly said.

"I didn't ask you," He glared at me for intervening.

"Nigga, what you better do is get the fuck from out of here," Kia snapped, and was walking towards his face, but the nigga pushed Kia into me, making us fall back on to the chairs behind us. He grabbed Heaven harshly and started dragging her towards the door. Kia and I tried to get up quickly as we watched Heaven try to fight him before she started screaming. Thank God her common sense kicked in. Kia and I rushed over to them and before we made it close by them, Ricardo came out of nowhere and punched him in the face, making him release Heaven. We grabbed Heaven and her face was stained with tears. Ricardo was beating Caleb's ass. He didn't have a chance. Heaven pulled away from us and rushed towards the fight.

"Stop! Stop! Ricardo you're going to kill him!" Heaven screamed. She was trying to pull Ricardo off him. "Please! Help me, Ricardo stop please!" She pleaded with him. Everyone stood around the fight no one wanted to interfere, some people even left. Ricardo stopped punching him and pushed Heaven back a little as he mugged her.

"Are you fucking serious? You taking up for this nigga? He been harassing you and knocking your shit loose, but you want me to stop!" Ricardo roared.

"Nooo Ric that's not it! I don't want you to go to jail! Please!" She pleaded.

"Jail! Jail! Man, I'll die about mine, the fuck you care about jail for? This nigga did all types of shit to you! I don't care about that shit!" Ricardo snapped.

"Aye man, I told you it was me or no one," Caleb said pulling out a gun. Shit happened so fast no one couldn't react in time.

"Noooo!!!" Heaven screamed moving in front of the bullets. She took three to the chest, before they knocked Caleb down.

"Heav!" Ricardo yelled as she fell back in his arms. I began to panic as Kia went straight into help mode. Kia began to put pressure on her chest.

"Amber! Snap out of it. Grab a tablecloth!" She yelled. I finally snapped out of my trance and took off towards the table. I heard people gasp and looked back to see Ricardo beating Caleb's ass.

"Did someone call 911!" Kia yelled out.

"They on the way!" Mack yelled coming over to Kia and took his jacket off and adding it to Heaven's chest as they tried to add all the pressure to her chest. Chase and Renzo pulled Ricardo up off Caleb because he was about to catch a murder for beating this nigga to death. I dropped down to the floor next to Kia. Heaven was gasping for air as her eyes rolled back.

"No, no, no!" Kia began to yell as she grabbed Heaven's face and the tears started to fall. I got so choked up, but when we heard more gunshots outside the front door and people ran back inside. Mack jumped up to run towards the door. We heard a bunch of commotion but was unsure of what happened. Looking back down at Heaven, I watched her body heave up and down, while Kia coaxed her to not close her eyes. When she finally took her last breath, the blood spilled out her mouth. Her eyes were just glossed, and her lifeless body was like dead weight.

"God please, No!" Kia screamed and we both just held on to her and cradled her together. My heart was broken. Her mom didn't come tonight because she wasn't feeling up to it, but the fact we had to deliver this news, I couldn't take it. The ambulance came in and got us to move out the way I felt like I was in a daze, but when Chase came back in with tears coming down his face with blood on him, and then he looked at Kia with this look.

"Kia, I'm sorry," Chase could barely get out.

"What's wrong Chase?" she yelled at him.

"Ol girl came out busting out of nowhere. Renzo was hit, but I don't know if he gon make it.

They rushed him out since he was still breathing,"
He managed to get the words out before Kia passed
out. I don't think this was the birthday we would
have ever expected. If Renzo died too, I knew that I
was going to have to be strong for Kia. Our family
have been through so much this was not expected. I
just knew everything was coming full circle and in a
good way.

IT'S OVER

Ricardo

Watching them put the black tarp over Heaven's body was something that could never leave my eyes. The fact she jumped in front of the gun that killed her to save my life will never leave my thoughts. I wake up in cold sweats every night because dream plays over and over in my head. I tried my best to kill him for what he did, but they stopped me. It was crazy how one of the officers wanted to take me to jail because he seen the watch I had on and felt like it was gang violence instead of what we told them over and over a fucking domestic dispute. It took an officer who wasn't the same color as me to really access the situation. That day is when my heart broke in a million pieces. That was the day, I lost love for ever. I don't think I would ever love anyone the way I loved Heaven. As hard as she was, she showed me how to persevere for what you want and don't let nothing stop you. I have always known Heaven and had a thing for her since Renzo started dating Kia, but I knew what type of women she was, so I waited till my shit was on point and everything was perfect when I asked her to be my realtor. I snuck in and stole her heart without her knowing.

I sat in the office that was supposed to be hers the one that sat in the building that was supposed to be hers. I couldn't help but let the tears fall. I decided to get my realty license and I am now in the works of getting my contracting license as well. A nigga was really good with his hands and flipping houses was easy to me. Leaving the whole life of running traps to open a realtor company that I named after Heaven was fulfilling because even though she stayed on my mind for a long time, I just knew me doing something that would make her be proud of me. It just made me go harder. Business was booming, but losing someone the way I did, I don't think you will ever feel complete in anything. There was an empty void in me that I just couldn't shake. I was about to walk out my office since it was six o'clock. I had this thing where I never stayed in the office past six and all employees had to be gone by five. I closed my door and turned around to see all the people I did still have sing Happy Birthday to me with a cake and candles. I smiled big as Little Renzo ran up to me.

"Happy birday unc" His little baby voice, did good saying the words.

"Make a wish," Amber said all smiles.

"Y'all know how I feel about this shit, man but I will do it," I blew the candles out. I had told them I didn't want to celebrate birthdays, even though it's been a little over a year since the day of Heaven's death. This my second birthday since the incident and I have been just fully committed into my business.

"We came with gifts," Kia said with a big smile. I knew she had been through a lot she took Heaven's death the hardest. Shit I think we all did. She handed me a bag and I took it from her.

"You know y'all didn't have to do that right?" I said to them.

"We know, we know," They all said in union.

"Just open it," My nephew said in his little voice annoyed with me taking so long. Opening the bag and removing the box, I got a little excited for the first time ever. I slowly opened the long jewelry box, and when my eyes landed on the pendant with a picture of me and Heaven all smiles on her birthday made a tear fall. This had to be the best birthday gift ever.

"Damn nigga you done became a little soft ass nigga," Renzo's voice made me look up, to see my brother in front me standing and walking towards me had to be the best gift ever. I grabbed him in a brotherly hug.

"Damn, my nigga when this happened?" I asked him.

"A few months ago. We just wanted to surprise you," He smiled.

"Now, that this shit done can we go to the booty club? A nigga wants some chicken wings and a dance," Chase's crazy ass said. Making us all laugh. Karina nudged him hard. "What? You coming too, baby," He pursed his lips up to her and she rolled her eyes and laugh.

"It's good seeing y'all man. A nigga been so busy," I said to everyone.

"Nigga, you be ignoring us and shit like we not helping you build this muthafucka here," Mack laughed. He was right, this was a group effort. I had all of them on payroll. Mack and Amber were a big help to my business because they have been doing this shit for a while now.

"How do you feel?" Kia asked me.

"Like a lucky man to have y'all as my family," I smiled big. I didn't have the woman I just knew was going to be my forever, but looking down at my pendant, she was still in my heart and for the first time ever, I felt like I could heal properly and was definitely going to take Kia's advice to see a therapist. Until next time y'all.

BETTER DAYS TO COME

Kia

The day Heaven died, I thought I lost my mind. When I woke up in the hospital and was told that Renzo was not going to make it, I just knew my life was not going to be right. I got on my knees and prayed that day like I never did before asking God to not take Renzo since he already got his Heaven. I guess what I said was enough for him, because after multiple surgeries he was still alive. They didn't think he would be able to do anything anymore. They told me was in a coma and not breathing on his own. They said his brain barely had activity because he lost oxygen for a long period of time. I spent days at the hospital not knowing if he was going to make it. I brought our son everyday even though they told me it wasn't a good idea. I wanted Renzo to hear his son cries or just feel his touch, just so he knew that we were waiting for him. This simple gesture was sure to give him the fight he needed.

I'm not going to lie it was a struggle going through that shit because I swear, I almost had to beat Sashay's ass again, because she was the so call mystery woman the nigga was talking to. The whole time I thought it was a new bitch, it was her weird ass. After catching her ass at the hospital for the fifth time, I had to understand why she was risking her life to come see him. When she broke it down how their relationship was, I told her I understood but made it noticeably clear to stay the hell away from him or next time she will be lying next to him. I guess she took heed to my warning because I haven't heard or seen the bitch anymore after that. I was very territorial during Renzo's healing. I didn't want no negative energy around him. I had faith he would wake up. I would never forget the day he did wake up. His baby would not stop crying, I mean he just wouldn't stop. I sat in the chair next to Renzo's bed as I held his little son and then I began to cry. I was stressed the fuck out. I was trying to do it all;

finish school, start up our own business and be a caretaker to two people. It's like fate had it for me. I was sitting in the bed and leaned forward as the tears fell. I felt Renzo's hand move to my hand. That day I was so fucking happy and been so into his damn care I don't think I slept. It was a long process, but after a little over a year, he was now walking and able to care for himself. I was more than happy I was grateful. God knew I couldn't lose another person in my life.

That day Nadia was watching us the whole time. Like she was real life stalking us in the same damn truck. When she shot at Renzo, he was the only one that took the bullets. She tried to leave, but Chase and Ricardo started shooting the tires out the truck. Her life was spared because the police pulled up in time before the boys could put a bullet in her. She was dragged to jail that night and is now still set for trial. Her silly ass wanted to take it to trial instead of taking the plea deal. They hit her ass with every charge they could think of when they discovered who her ass was. I swear I think her family gave her up just so they didn't have to deal with the backlash from the police and anyone who had dealings with her. She was hit with a Rico, racketeering, distribution, trafficking attempted murder and murder charges. I knew Lolita could have gotten her out, but because she was overseeing everything, and Vinny was still ill. It was her way or no way, and if you ask me, I think something was up with Vinny not being healthy enough to run his business, but that was no longer my concern. With Renzo being down, everyone went their separate ways. The only person who was still running wild in these streets was Chase. He was young and still had the drive for hustling whereas all of us had enough.

"You ready to slide?" Renzo said once we were in the car settled. We had just come from seeing Ricardo to wish him a happy birthday. I looked up at his building and seeing *Heaven's Haven Realty* made me smile. The fact he dedicated this building to her, was amazing. He started a foundation for domestic violence in her memory and was in a mentor program for young men. I was proud of how far he came, and I couldn't wait to see what was next.

"Yea, she would have been so happy if she would have had this place to herself," I said admiring the building.

"Yea I could hear her ass crying through the speaker phone begging for shit." We laughed. "Sorry, if I ever took you for granted, and I promise that from here on out a nigga will do right," Renzo expressed. I knew he was serious because I heard him tell his brother on the phone plenty times how much he appreciated me. I couldn't lie, we were closer than ever before, and I had to admit all that hate I had for him was gone. I was happy he was ok, and we were thriving as a family. All the time he spent home recovering, he got into stocks. With my help he became really good at it. He started flipping his money from home, while I assisted him with his therapy, I found a new love and decided to switch my major again. I could see Heaven laughing at me for doing the shit again, but helping Renzo made me realize how much I loved helping with physical therapy. I was close to being finished and I couldn't wait for my next journey in life because I was finally excited about completing something.

"Love you Renzo," I simply said to him. He grabbed my hand and kissed the back of it as we drove home. I learned a valuable lesson in life and that was to never take it for granted and appreciate every moment of it.

THINGS NEVER
CHANGE

Amber

While everyone had somewhat a happy
ending since Heaven died, it's me who is still stuck
in this stupid ass situation with Mack. Tina had this
so call baby, but I swear the baby looks nothing like
his ass and he just refuses to DNA this fucking
baby. It's me who got tired of the drama between
them two and decided to start back fucking Troy. So
now I'm in a shit show of fucking drama. That night
of Heaven's death you would have thought it would
have brought me and Mack closer. In fact it made
me go further away from him. I was scared to shit
for Tina's silly ass to turn psycho on me. Shit Nadia
shot Renzo, Caleb shot Heaven; like people don't
play about their hearts and after I already did that
shit to Tina a few years back, I just knew if I did
some shit to her now, she would try and off me.

Mack was not feeling me trying to move on. He would pop up on me and act crazy, but I ignored him constantly until the day Tina gave birth. I just knew when we saw the baby, he knew it wasn't his child. Well, that didn't happen. This fool embraced this baby like it came from his nut sac. I just knew after seeing this baby, I was going to have my man back, but after he didn't question the paternity, I knew this nigga either loved her or was dumb. I'm not going to lie though, Mack never let up and I tried so hard to stay out of his way, but with us owning a business together, it was hard for him to keep it strictly business at times. Mack was always trying to be up my ass. Just like now when we came to see Ricardo for his birthday, the nigga had to jump in the car with me. So, now I'm stuck riding around with his silly ass and that's just fucking annoying.

"So, damn you not going to dead this shit with you and that nigga?" Mack said pointing at my ringing phone in the cup holder. Realizing it was Troy I rolled my eyes.

"Listen, Mack we will never work as long as Tina is your kid's mother and because that isn't changing, we can't be in no relationship," I truthfully told him.

"So, what happens when I'm the father of your child?" He seriously said, and I burst into laughter.

"Nigga I have to be pregnant, and that's not happening," I laughed so hard. I grabbed my phone and began texting Troy because we had a date planned.

"Really, you think the shit funny? So let me ask you then who would be the daddy?" Mack calmly asked, as he drove my car back to our office.

"Mack, what is you talking about?" I curiously asked, with a frown on my face.

"If you were pregnant, who would be the father?" he asked looking at me and then back at the road.

"Nigga, are you serious right now?" I questioned and he stared at me like bitch answer the question. I rolled my eyes because I honestly didn't feel like entertaining the question he was asking. I finished sending my message and put my phone down, but when pregnancy test fell in my lap and hit my phone screen my heart fell in my ass. Did this nigga go through my fucking trash?

"Mack, what the fuck is this?" I tried to play it off.

"Hmph, so is it Troy's baby or mine?" he asked. I just sat there because honestly, I knew exactly who baby it was, but I had plans to get rid of it. I was not ready to be no one's mother. I knew if I told Mack the truth, I would be having a baby, so I did what was best for me in that moment and that was lie.

"Troy's," I simply said. His jawline flexed and the vein on the side of his head began to pulsate.

"Aiight, cool so when the baby is born, we will say it's mine," he said as if I was keeping it.

"What makes you think I want it?" I asked him.

"I know you don't, but Amber you're a horrible liar and a niggas not dumb. I know that's my baby, but since you want to play dumb, we can wait this shit out together," He simply said.

"What? You can't make me keep a baby, and definitely since your ass is in denial about the one you just had with Tina," I frowned my face up.

"You always fussing about Tina, but a nigga be around you all the fucking time and if I'm not, I'm fucking home. I even bring the kids with me so you won't feel no way. Why are you always fighting a nigga? Like I was cool with us fucking, I was cool with you not wanting to be in a relationship, I was cool with you messing with that weak ass nigga Troy, I was cool with you doing you, but this shit has got to fucking stop," Mack pleaded with me, but I wasn't feeling shit he was saying. Since he wanted to do sneaky shit, I did my own shit. Going in my purse, I pulled out the envelope. I tore it open and read the results out loud to him. When he looked over at me and seeing how serious I was. He smashed on the brakes, making my head hit the dashboard.

"You can't be serious right now. Get the fuck out Amber!" He bellowed making me jump. Not waiting to see what this nigga was about to do, I grabbed my shit and phone and got the fuck out the car leaving the paternity test of both his kids. Not sure what DNA specialist they went too, but the bitch lied about the first one and lied about the second child too. I decided to do a DNA test on both kids since I was already swabbing one. I swear I thought the first child was his, but whoever did the DNA the bitch must have knew them because I was shocked to hear the results for his daughter. When Mack sped off past me, leaving me on the street, I wasn't mad because I could only imagine what Tina was about to endure. I went inside my phone and requested a Lyft because at that moment I was not going to Troy's. Thinking about the outcome of shit I just did and what could happen I quickly called Mack's phone because I needed to make sure he didn't do nothing stupid. He picked up but didn't say anything. Hearing the car sound like it was speeding, I began to talk to him. I had to go against what I wanted to be sure the nigga didn't do nothing crazy.

"Mack, baby I'm sorry for DNA testing the kids. I just needed to know the truth. Please go home. I will go home if you go. Think about all the shit you have to lose. Going over there to Tina will not make the kids yours and it will only hurt more," I tried talking him down. He sniffed hard like he was crying and at that moment I felt so bad. My own selfish reasons caused me to hurt him again. I had walked over to a nearby gas station, but when I saw Mack pull up on the side of me, I thanked God he didn't do nothing crazy. I hung up my phone and canceled my Lyft ride. I got into the car and for the first time ever I saw him break down as I tried to wrap my small arms around him. I immediately apologize over and over because I took something away from him. Once he calmed down, I wiped his tears with my hand and gave him a reassuring peck on the cheek.

"Mack how did you know where I was?" I curiously asked he looked at me and smirked.

"Amber, your location is always shared with me. I know where you at, at all times," he drove off from the gas station as if he didn't just tell me so crazy ass shit.

"You know what? Out of all this shit, I can say one thing shit just never change with us, we gon always have some crazy shit going on," I laughed and so did he.

After that day Mack and I had a deep conversation about everything we had going on and thought it was best to take it one day at a time. I did cut all ties with Troy to try and focus on us and he decided to tell Tina about the paternity results of both kids. She was so mad that she tried to do everything in her power to manipulate the situation. I swear Mack and I always had to just get ourselves together for the next show of drama in our lives because shit just never changes.

THE END.

NOTE FROM THE AUTHOR

If you are reading this, that means you made it through the journey of drama and emotions in this book. I know it has been a while, in the anticipation for this part 3, but I just wanted to make sure I gave you guys something good and of quality. I promise my next series I will not keep you waiting too long. Thank you for riding with me this long and being an Avid or new reader of mine. I appreciate each and every one of you. If you want to be updated on any current/ new releases or just to simply reach out to me, follow me on:

Facebook: Authoress Lexi-B

Instagram: Lexib_authoress

Made in the USA
Monee, IL
23 July 2021